Angels and Guitars

10/06
Annette Carolyn Ely
(Cordes)

Annette Carolyn Ely

HEINS PUBLICATIONS, INC.
Eau Claire Wisconsin
U.S.A.

First Published September, 2006

ISBN 0-9748680-6-X

Published in the USA by
HEINS PUBLICATIONS
Rev. William A. Heins
2016 Leonard Ct.
Eau Claire WI 54703-9000
Tel. # 715.874.6677 or 1.800.55HEINS
email: revheins@heins.com

To the Fosters

with

love.

TABLE OF CONTENTS

Angels and Guitars

"There lives and works
a soul in all things,
and that soul
is God."

William Cowper (1731-1800)
-by-
Leading English Poet of domesticity and humanitarianism; thought to write the most intimately charming letters of that day.

Chapter 1

Cousins

Minnesota was wearing its summer finery. Orange poppies, lavender violets, pink, red, and yellow roses vied for attention with the multi-colored sweet peas in Grandma Annie's garden. The fragrant little faces seemed to smile up at the elderly woman when she picked them for they knew that a sick mother, or child and possibly an elderly person in the nursing home would receive them as a gift in about an hour's time. The lilies especially liked being picked. They knew that they would grace the altar in church at the foot of the Christ who had His hands stretched out in blessing toward all who gathered there to pray.

Little Annie was at Grandmother's this particular morning.

"Oh! let me do it!" Annie was hopping up and down in excitement watching Grandma pump the handle to get water from the old well under the horse-chestnut tree. The elder laughed as Annie continued: "I need to use both hands to pull the handle down, but if you'll let me do it, I'll pump water for you until I'm ONE HUNDRED YEARS OLD!"

"I can't pass up a good offer like that!" Grandma declared. Watching her granddaughter swing up and down on the red lever made her chuckle harder, let alone the thought that Annie took for granted she'd live to be a hundred!

"Annie, if you live to be one hundred, I'll be one hundred and fifty six!"

"That's okay. I'll love you anyway," the child chirped.

"Come on, Annie," Grandmother laughed, "let's go into the house and count the money in your Missionary-to-Africa can. It must be getting quite heavy by now. Before you know it, we'll be waving good-bye to you at the pier in New Orleans or New York."

"Oh, Grandma!" Annie laughed. "I can't go that fast. I have to grow up first."

By that time, they had reached the dining room hutch where the red Folger's coffee can was kept in a drawer. Opening it, Grandmother Anne lifted the bank out. "My, but this feels light," she exclaimed. Opening the lid, the silver bottom winked up at them. There were only two dimes, one nickel, and a penny. Grandma looked quizzically at her namesake.

"Grandma," Annie whispered. "Don't tell anybody, but the devil got into it." She looked furtively around the room.

"Seems to me that if the devil got into it, the can would be pretty heavy. He's a big fellow, you know," Grandma teased.

A blush stole over Annie's face and neck.

"Are you sure he's in there?" the kind woman enquired.

"Weeell-he's bad, you know, Grandma," Annie demurely replied.

"That he is. Maybe he isn't in there at all. Maybe there just isn't much money in it yet. If a girl hasn't had many good paying jobs this summer, there wouldn't be much to put into the coffee can. Should we go into the house, make lemonade and sell a few glasses to Mr. Tan when he passes by at noon?" Grandma smiled.

"Oh, Grandma! You're the smartest lady in the world! I'd like that very much!" Annie's face lifted with happiness. "Daddy would call you a blessing!"

"How so, child?" Grandma's eyes twinkled.

"Well, I prayed and asked God to forgive me." Annie took a breath.

"Forgive you for what, dear?"

"To forgive me for using a nickel every time I came to town."

"You mean you used five cents each visit, from your missionary can?"

"Yes," honest Annie replied.

Suddenly Grandmother remembered

giving Annie baking soda in water the night before when the girl complained of a tummy ache.

The candy counter at the dime store loomed largely in Grandma's neat head. "What did you say you had used the money for?" Grandmother asked.

"Well, I bought cherry drops for you and caramels for me. Then, I walked all the way to your house, but I stopped to watch the doves in the park. Before you know it...the bag was empty! Just like that!" Annie tried to snap her fingers the way her brother Jan did. Trying to make thumb and middle finger click, she quite forgot her recent shame.

Grandma laughed to see the child's head at an angle, tongue held between teeth while trying to imitate her oldest brother.

"Oh, come on Annie," she took the girl's little hand. "Let's go make lemonade and earn a few coins for that can of yours! At the rate the money is going in and coming out of it, you'll have to take a loan to get to Africa!"

"What's a loan, Grandma?" Annie squinted up at her.

For a reply, Granny just laughed.

An hour and twenty cents later, a satisfied Mr. Tan and a happy girl went their separate ways as Granny grinned from the dining room window. Later, watching her namesake add nickels to the Folgers tin, the joy of being a grandmother flooded her heart.

"God answered my prayer," Annie smiled up at the local genius. Anne lifted the lid off the container, listened to four distinct clinks as Buffalo coins dropped into its depths, giving rise to faith in her grandchild's heart. Little Blondie continued, "Jesus helped me earn twenty cents back!"

"Do you think you'll be able to keep it in there?" the matriarch asked as she tapped the can.

"If I leave it here, and you hide it, the money will stay inside becauthe old Beezlbub won't know where to find it." Annie pointed to the top of Grandmother's spoolshelf in the corner. "It reaches almost to the ceiling, and even if I stand on your sewing machine, I won't be able to reach the money when I want a piece of candy from the store."

"Where did you hear that name?" Granny laughed.

"Daddy calls him that," Annie said.

"I'm sure he says Bealzebub," Granny hadn't stopped chuckling. "Now remember, child, don't try to climb the shelves because you will pull the furniture over onto yourself. Will you think of that when you get hungry for a sweet?" Grandma looked soberly at Annie.

Silently, Annie looked up with somber green eyes.

"I'll tell you what you can do if temptation overwhelms you, Annie. Come here." She took the girl's fingers and led her into the kitchen. "See the stool in the corner by the cookie jar?" She pointed at a square seat with a sturdy leather top and four inch legs which were almost as wide as they were tall. "Fetch that stool and bring it here, please."

Annie picked it up and went to stand beside her mentor who was standing at kitchen cupboards which hung over an extended cabinet.

"You may set it down." Grandmother indicated a spot. Annie set the tiny stool down and looked up again.

"Hop onto the stool, and open the cupboard door nearest the windows."

Annie did as she was bid.

"What do you see?" Grandma's emerald peepers danced.

"I see caramels and cherry drops in a glass dish with a lid on it!" Annie squealed.

"Go ahead and have one." Grandma lifted the lid off the candy dish. Annie stuck her lemon soaked fingers into the glorious concoction, capturing a soft, red cherry ball. Popping it into her mouth she turned to look at her beloved heroine who knew how to solve EVERY problem!

"When you yearn for a candy, you are allowed to get one piece of whichever kind you choose. But then you must be a good girl and refrain from getting your coffee can! Will you do that for me?" Mrs. Illy asked.

"I sure hope so!" Annie exclaimed, smacking her lips around the cherry juice which threatened to make a red line down her chin.

"I need to know that you will or I'll have to hide both the can AND the candy dish from sight. I hate to do that. You see, I believe that all of us can learn to have a treat when it is the proper time. I also believe that all of us can learn to have a special time for treats."

Annie's eyes explored the ceiling. She saw a fly standing upside down like Fred Astaire in a movie her aunt, who owned the movie theatre downtown, talked about. She wasn't allowed to go to movies, so she didn't know if that was a true story or not. It sounded pretty fishy. 'But if flies can walk on the ceiling, why can't people?' she thought. She'd have to try it sometime.

"When it comes to money we donate to God - such as your money in the red can, dear," Annie heard her grandma drone on, "we shouldn't use it once we've given it to Him."

"Oh," Annie said when she heard Grandma take a breath. In the girl's head she was thinking she'd better wear slacks when trying to walk upside-down, and put glue on the bottoms of her shoes.

That fly sure was taking his sweet time on Grandma's ceiling!

"Annie, are you listening?" gently chided Anne.

Annie tore her eyes from the winged black insect to look at her pal.

"All I'm saying is that you gave to God, so now I'm giving to you. That way you don't have to borrow what you gave Him." Grandma couldn't help but laugh at the quizzical look in her preoccupied grandchild's eyes. "Do you think you can keep from climbing up to get the red can?" the older woman asked.

"That's a tough call to make, Grandma," Annie complained. "When I'm hungry, I'd rather have candy than set sail for Africa! Can't we sell lemonade until I leave to help the lost, if we need to?" she added.

Grandma started to laugh, and said, "Child, if you are that hungry, eat a sandwich. Candy is just a treat. We mustn't fill up on it. And yes, we can sell more lemonade."

"Why is delithuth thtuff just a treat?" Annie started lisping.

"Because candy has no lasting food value as do sandwiches and fruit. You want to eat well in order to grow strong muscles and a smart brain."

"I see," Annie murmured. "Okay, I give up! I'll eat just one piece of candy, and eat the sandwich," her nose wrinkled a bit. Her lisp waned with a made-up mind.

"And?" her Grandma asked.

"And, I won't climb up the shelves to get the can."

"Good. That's what I wanted to hear. I know that I won't have to worry about it, you are such a good girl."

"What if someone else climbs up?"

Annie inquired. She was already thinking of soliciting Trisha's aid.

"Who do you mean...Grandpa? The shelf is in the bedroom, you know, and I don't think he'll be climbing the shelves anytime soon, dear. He doesn't even climb trees to hunt deer anymore." Mrs Illy was laughing again. "No, my little one. The coffee can is safe with us. Once it is full you can take it to the bank and into your missionary account it will go!"

"But, I thought I was giving the money to God, not the bank! Besides, Daddy says that old Mr. Norlund takes every interested penny he can! Will my nickels be interested, too?" Annie was getting defensive.

"No, no, darling!" Grandma scooped her up and twirled her around the room. "Daddy means that when one borrows money from the bank, they have to be paid for the borrower using it. That's called 'interest'. The interest is usually high, meaning it takes every penny one can scrape together sometimes. But, you won't be borrowing dear. You will be saving your earnings, and the bank will pay YOU interest for leaving it there."

"Well, I don't know. What if one of them wants a cherry drop and they forget their own money at home?" Annie dubiously inquired.

"Don't worry. No one will use it because it's against the law." Grandma soothed. "When the end of the year comes, they will add money to yours for you being such a good girl as to leave it there. They won't steal the missionary money."

"By the time I'm an old lady like Mama, I'll be able to go to Africa, right?" Annie asked as thoughts of Trisha climbing up the shelves after the cache suddenly held greater appeal.

*

One day the telephone rang at the farm house. Daisy answered.

Annie heard sounds like a duck coming through the receiver which was at Daisy's ear.

"I see," her mother responded. "When will they arrive?" The cheerful duck kept quacking over the wires. Annie knew it was Aunt Vanilla.

"Why, of course they can stay here! Annie and the rest of the kids will be delighted. You know how they love their uncle Sam and Aunt Lila's kids! Our roof will be hopping up and down from all the giggles and happiness Sammy and Cherry will bring!"

Annie's little heart felt like it was going to burst with joy! She guessed from listening to her mom's side of the conversation that her cousins were coming up from Nebraska again. They came every summer without fail to stay at Grandma and Grandpa's house.

Actually, they came to stay at the farm just as often as in town at Grandma's. Annie thought she'd die of thrills on the spot! She started dancing up and down on her toes, braids flying in rhythm, wispy curls escaping in tendrils around her neck and forehead.

Mama hung the receiver onto the telephone, a shiny oak box on the wall that had two, black, upside down cups with a metal stick in the middle for a bell. When that stick whacked out four long dings, Annie had learned that more nice things happened! Now her cousins were coming. She was so happy, she wished to kiss the telephone but kissed her mother instead, scrambling onto a chair to do it. After all, the telephone couldn't kiss her back, couldn't hug either; and it didn't smell deliciously of English lavender like Daisy.

"I thought that would make you happy, Annie," her mother said warmly. "The way you love Cherry, it worries me sometimes. Of course, she's a wonderful girl, and you couldn't have a better idol, I suppose. I know that you are safe when you are with her even though she is three years older and could make quite a precocious child of you."

"What's precothuth?" Annie squinted against the sunshine streaming through the kitchen window.

"Being too grown up for your age, darling," her mom gave her a squeeze. "Now, get down and let's go pick green beans for dinner."

"Oh," Annie's face fell ten feet to the basement. "Do I have to?"

"Do you want to eat?" Daisy countered.

"Yeth," came a muted response, "but I won't eat any beanth if I don't have to pick them. That way you won't have to pick tho many and hurt your back." Eyebrows were raised in question over green eyes as a determined smile touched Annie's lips. Anything to get out of sticking one's hand into a clingy cobweb, or onto a garden snake as it slept beneath the cool shade! She hated both almost to the point of terror.

"Don't lisp, darling," Daisy said.

"And anyway, why can't the hired girl

do it?" a bolder-by-the-second Annie demanded.

"Do you remember the story of the little red hen?" her mother quickly asked.

Annie saw no tempest in a teapot brewing in her mother's countenance, so said, "No?" inflecting her voice up as if in a question.

"Then, let me read it to you. It won't take long," her mother guided her to the living room where she set Annie on her lap while pulling a Mother Goose book from the end table.

Annie smiled. 'I got out of that one,' she thought.

Her mother read the story to a very interested daughter.

As the reading became more involved, Annie felt herself sympathizing with the mother hen whose naughty chicks wouldn't help her gather the wheat, beat the grain from the stalks of wheat, winnow the chaff out from the heads of the grain, grind the newly cleaned harvest into flour, nor even help bake the bread! But when it came time to answer their noses when sweet aromas wafted from the kitchen, ALL of them were eagerly waiting around the honey pot and butter dish, knives in hand to lather both generously on thick slices of warm golden goodness!

"Mama!"

Daisy looked down at her daughter who was peering up at her with a storm of indignation in her emerald eyes.

"Yes, dear?" the Mother purred, knowing already what was going to be said, for, she knew her Annie. She had a little spirit which demanded justice once a matter was thought out.

"Those lazy chicks. What's wrong with them anyway!"

Daisy laughed. "Probably the same thing that is wrong with you right now."

Annie really became indignant, and spouted, "I'm <u>not</u> lazy like them!" She sat bolt upright and looked her mom squarely in the eye.

"Oh?" Her mom closed the book.

Annie suddenly lost her imperious

manner, and blushed.

"Yes, I am," she was almost in tears. "I don't want to help you pick the beans for supper." She looked in anguish at her pretty, raven-haired mother.

"Might you have changed your mind by now?" Mrs. Cummings softly wondered aloud. "They certainly taste good smothered in butter. The mashed potatoes and gravy with baked chicken compliments them, too, I always thought. What do you think?" She shifted Annie's weight on her lap, "not to mention the strawberries and whipped cream over angel food cake I've made for those who eat everything on their dinner plates."

Now, there wasn't anything Annie loved to eat more than the very things mentioned, including the string beans. But, she knew that her appetite would keenly suffer if she made Mama go out to the garden alone to gather them. After all, she was a big girl now - big enough to have gotten saved and baptized last spring. She was at what her father called 'the age of accountability', that age when a child knows right from wrong. She now knew that it was wrong not to help her mother gather food for the evening meal.

"Mom, if I help you pick beans, it's because I'm old enough to do it, right?"

"Right."

"Well, do you think I am old enough to make dinner tomorrow noon? I could stand on a chair and you could show me how to use the real stove," Annie reasoned. She rarely gave in on one point without obtaining a return favor. Her uncle said that one had to 'parley' in life, and that was how it was done!

"Hmmm. I don't know, you're quite young to stand by the hot burners, dear."

"But if I promise to be careful, and wear an apron, and you stay beside me the whole time, I'll do everything you say. I won't get burned. I promise."

"What do you want to prepare?" her mother asked, suddenly realizing that when opportunity knocks, one should take it even in the raising of one's children. Apparently,

Annie was ready since she had thought it out even as to her own safety.

"Could we fix the sunfish Grandpa caught yesterday?"

"If they're not green by now," Daisy laughed.

"Oh, Mama!" Annie nodded her head. "They're in the freezer!"

"Okay, I'll teach you how to roll them in flour and fry them slowly in butter to a crisp on the outside and succulence on the inside!" her mother agreed.

"What's succulence?" Annie wanted to know.

"Oh, come on, moppet," her mom said as she bounced Annie off her knee, and swatted her derriere playfully, "let's go pick beans. The last one to the garden is a donkey's tail!" With that her mom sprinted out of the house and down the garden path with Annie hot on her heels, calling, "Wait for me!"

Chapter 2

Buried Treasure

"To be or not to be, that is the question!" Sammy stood on the sawed off tree trunk in the pasture, one chubby finger held up in the air over his yellow hair, his round chest and stomach clothed in a blue T-shirt with white lines sailing around and around the fabric as if to make Annie, his adoring audience, dizzy. His blue jeans were new, and still quite clean considering that they had just crawled through the hay up in the haymow to find the kittens after fending off the spitting mother cat. Petting the darling little things whose eyes weren't open yet, the kids then went to the hole in the middle of the haymow floor and jumped down through the opening into a huge pile of fragrant alfalfa. Midst shrieks and happy laughter, they joined Jan and Reginald in climbing the ladder into the nervous mother cat's maternity ward.

They jumped again and again. Finally, one feline's nervous breakdown later, and four heads full of white clover blossoms, they all lay wondering what they could do next. The kittens had been pulled onto their chests to be petted. They felt so soft to Annie.

"I know what!" an indefatigable eight-and-a-half-year-old Nebraskan said as he sat up.

"What?" drawled Reginald.

"Yes, what, Sammy," Annie giggled. Sammy had a tuft of hay sticking out of a cowlick at the back of his head and didn't know it. SHE wasn't going to tell! That, plus his belly hanging out of his T-shirt made her laugh for there was chaff in the tummy button, too.

Sammy looked at her wondering what was so funny. But he liked Annie, so let her laugh. Girls were weird anyway - but for a girl, she wasn't half shabby! It was fun to scare her with bullfrogs, a favorite pastime which he was loathe to give up years down the pike when he was the ripe old age of fifteen. Now he was an indomitable eight, almost nine, and full of fun which suited his age.

"We could shimmy up the fir tree outside the dining room window and sit on top," the wizard of the midwestern state said. "Or, hot diggety-dog, we could look for Uncle Malvern's hidden treasure that he buried by the tepees! He and his brothers put it there when they were kids."

"We did that yesterday," Annie announced, her voice sounding bored.

"Anyway, Annie hates worms," Jan said.

Sammy chuckled thinking of Annie squealing over an angleworm.

"Well, then, we could go out to the pond in the west pasture and play cowboys and Indians in the tepees! Those guys sure built nice ones! Look, you can see both of them from here!" Sammy exclaimed.

Annie wrinkled her nose. "There might be skunks in them," she shivered. "And the tepees leak! Remember two nights ago when we slept there, and the storm came? We almost drowned when the rain poured through the cracks!"

"Yeh, we had to hold an umbrella over our blankets," Reggie agreed, "and the puddle under the plastic mattress got so high, we floated."

A beaut of a smile lit Sammy's face as if he had seen all of heaven come down. He chuckled, "Did you see the big snake that was swimming under your bed in the puddle, Annie?" Of course, he was making it up.

Annie went pale.

"There was no snake, moppet, he's just teasing you," Jan gently comforted.

"Whew! That was a close call," his little sister heaved a sigh of relief, scooting closer to her big brother.

"I don't like snakes, Sammy," Annie looked trustingly at her cousin.

"But, wouldn't a nice green necklace that wiggled be envied by all your friends at school?" Sammy teased.

"If she wasn't pale enough before, now Annie's chalk white, Sammy. It isn't right to scare people out of their wits," elder Jan kindly admonished his mischievous cousin.

"I guess you're right," Sammy agreed. "After all, I don't care for snakes much myself!" A silent thought popped into his head.

'Now a frog. That's a different story! She's too sweet to chase with creepy crawlers. But a hopper, that's a definite possibility!' He grinned impishly and said, "Well, Annie, this time I'll chase the snakes away from you if you'll play with us by the tepees. But, I don't know what's so bad about garden snakes. They won't bite you. Besides, they eat bugs and mosquitoes. They're our friends."

"I don't like that kind of friend. You can have them. I've got other friends, like the kitties and Aunt Vanilla's canary in her kitchen." No two ways about it, Annie did NOT like insects, vermin, toads or frogs.

"You don't even like angleworms," Sammy laughed, not unkindly. "You're a pansy, but you're OUR pansy, so I guess that's alright." He chuckled until his belly shook like a bowl of jelly which made his shirt come unstuck and slide down to the waist of his jeans.

"Well, are you with us, or not?" Reginald asked Annie.

"Do you all swear not to chase me with snakes, toads, frogs, or the like?" she dubiously asked. "Cross your heart, hope to die and stick a needle in your eye?"

"We're not supposed to swear, Annie, but we'll promise...for today," Reggie said.

Sammy didn't say anything.

"And," Annie continued imperiously now that she had seemingly won the battle, "if I play cowboys I get to be a GIRL this time, like Dale Evans!" She tossed her head.

"Okay, be a sissy girl. I'm going to be Black Bart!" Reggie announced.

Jan laughed, "And I'll be Moses in the bulrushes."

"I'll be Wyatt Earp," Sammy pretended he threw up, "and I'll chase you all out of Dodge!" The Nebraskan continued, "Dodge is in Kansas close to where I live you know. We're westerner's. You're just tenderfoots."

"Wanna bet?" Reggie bristled. "The Dalton gang used to rob banks in Minnesota. We're no yellow bellies!"

"Wait! Wait!" Annie started hopping up and down in the hay. "If we play boy stuff, will you play Fairy Princess with me afterward?"

Even Jan couldn't keep from howling in objection to that one.

"Well then, how about playing 'Preacher' with me?" she did a cartwheel. She never could get her knees straightened out once they left the ground, like Trisha.

"Hey! That might be fun!" Sammy decided. "I think it was a great preacher who said a few choice words, and I'll teach them to you."

That's how the kids ended up in the meadow, Sammy standing on a tree stump repeating Shakespeare, whom he thought was the greatest preacher who had ever lived since Jesus.

"But, I thought he was a poet, Daddy said," Annie blushed at the look Sammy gave her. You know, as if to ask, "Are you stupid, or what?"

"On second thought," Sam, the fair-minded (for that he was) said, "Maybe he was a yarn rhythmer-poet or preacher, what's the difference? They both stand on a stage and get everyone's attention. And, they get paid for it, too. They don't even have to WORK!"

Reginald stood up. "Oh God, please let me be a preacher or poet," he implored, looking heavenward with zeal.

CRASH!

He fell over backwards flat on his back in supplication.

Peals of laughter rolled from the kids.

"Since you want to be one of those, I'll show you how," Sammy said. "Then we can all take turns practicing on this stump."

Sammy hopped up, right foot forward to scale the podium. He missed and plopped flat on his face. "Oops!" he laughed, "I guess I won't be able to join the circus as an acrobat," he giggled in his infectious way.

"You could be a clown," Annie earnestly consoled.

"Oh, shut up, Annie," Reggie said.

"You're not supposed to say 'shut up!'" Annie shot back. "Shame on you. Wait 'til Mama hears about that!" Her dignity had been compromised. A fierce scowl made her chubby cheeks look like pears - all bunched up around a puckered mouth.

Into the squabble came a serenely spoken, "To be or not to be, that is the question." Sammy had gained the perch, and was standing like Napoleon with right hand tucked down his T-shirt neck, ripping it along the way, left hand in the air, pointer finger aimed at heaven, a silly grin spread across his purposely idiotic face.

Jan, Annie and Reggie dissolved into

gales of giggles. They didn't know it at the time, but they had heard the greatest bard's of all time most famous line.

It sounded romantic and mysterious to Annie who ALWAYS was donning her sister's skirts and mother's mantilla, drop earrings, and necklaces to play princess. Why, even her favorite funny-paper strip was Sir Oaky Doaks and Princess Pamona! She was certain that they were real people and Sammy's recitation fit her imagination perfectly. When her mom had made a pointed hat onto which she attached a mantilla for Annie to float about the castles of her mind in play, the only thing which had ruined that particular day was when Reggie had asked why she was wearing a dunce cap.

Now, here was her adored and very wise, worldly cousin spouting something that soothed her challenged 'old soul.' He was laying ancient but everlastingly beautiful flowers of thought in her little mind. She liked it even better than when her dad quoted "Abou Ben Adam," or "The Village

Smith". Her mirth ceased, and she watched Sammy wax serious as he launched into his 'sermon' for the day!

"Dearly beloved, we are gathered together to witness," he quickly made up something because of not knowing the rest, "a hairy ape and a big animal with a hose up its nose, an elephant! The question is: Are we going to have an elephant in our town? Is it to be, or not to be! THAT is the question!"

"Oh, get down and let's play cowboys and Indians, Sammy," Reginald implored. "Better yet, let's go ask Mama if she'll take us swimming!"

"But, I thought we were going to dig for Uncle Lennie and Daddy's treasure," Annie pouted.

"Well, we need spades, sweetie," Jan consoled as he thought he heard a twig snap. "Let's go swimming first and then bring shovels back with us." He looked around at the meadow, but saw nothing unusual.

Beady eyes peered at them through

long, scraggly branches of the paw-paw thicket which grew beyond the tepees.

With shouts of approval they all marched along black cowpaths under shady elms toward the brown farmhouse. Annie looked up at a gray squirrel, stepping directly into a mess.

Sammy spied a bull-frog, but not before sharp-eyed Annie. She was already halfway toward the safety of her mother in the big house by the time he saw it. His little cousin was running as if the very devil were at her heels, dirty shoes and all. All living things cleared the trail. Annie's scent was something fierce!

"Oh, well, there's always a tomorrow," Sammy chuckled as he watched her run. He passed the frog with a wink of one blue eye as if there were a pact between them regarding Annie. After all, the bullfrog wanted Annie to like him, too. Wasn't he one of God's creatures as well?

Bleary blues of a hidden trespasser watched the four kids scamper toward the buildings; and then, plodding from behind the bushes to the wigwams, the man started poking vulnerable patches of soft earth with a stick. Leaves and twigs twisted from the trees during storms were scooted this way and that by the industrious search.

"I wonder just how much money is buried here?" he asked no one in particular. "I suppose Mal's parents buried it during the Depression."

Working diligently for awhile with the pine stick, he soon tired and decided, "Shoot! Why not let the kids do all the hard work. If I wait, they'll dig it up for me!"

With that in mind, the skinny little fellow went slogging through the slough, brown shoes and all to his black car which waited on the county road beyond the woods.

*

The next day was Sunday, and once again, the goslings followed the gander to the clapboard church in town, all except Sammy and Cherry, who if they went at all, attended the Methodist church down the street with Grandmother Illy.

Being ferried in style on the back seat of Grandfather's blue Cadillac was a treat in itself. Sammy and Cherry were Lutherans, the Illy's were Methodists and the Cummings were Baptists. No one from the outside looking in at the familial dynamics of these three groups would have guessed it because they all got along so well and had so much fun together. Their motto was, "If you love the Lord Jesus, good for you. You're my buddy! I don't care in which church you pray."

But Annie secretly wished all summer that she, too, could go with Grandma Illy, Sammy and Cherry to the Methodist church until her cousins went back to Nebraska in late August. Besides that, she had friends from that church who came to visit when Mal practiced with a quartet who sang on the radio and at various functions throughout the state.

"But, what would I do without Trish at church?" she wondered, and let it go at that. "And then there's Brysie, and my new friend, Wernadine. Nope, I'd better be satisfied. They need me to sing with Trish at the Old Folks home, anyway."

She sighed, "It's not easy being six years old!"

Chapter 3

The Stalker

Two years had gone by and with it Annie's baby teeth, the consequent spaces left when they had come out, and her lisp. She was very happy that no longer could Reggie call her pumpkin head. She felt quite grown up indeed.

During the past winter, Annie had developed a special attachment with a young man in the senior youth group of the little Swedish Baptist church. He soon became a second daddy to Annie because they were thrown together during quartet practices which her parents hosted or attended at other singers homes.

Ronald Foerster was the only son of

her Sunday School teacher. He had a beautiful tenor voice. It was as heavenly as his mother's and sister's voices. The women, of Swedish descent, sang high soprano as wondrously as Jenny Lind, the Swedish Nightingale. Annie always thought they were angels sent from heaven just to sing and couldn't wait to hear them on weekends. When Ronald joined them, harmonizing while playing his electric guitar, Annie thought she had died and gone to heaven! To fall under the spell of their gifts in song was one of Annie's favorite things.

One Sunday when a blizzard had made the Cumming's quarter mile driveway impassable, Ronald had driven from town to their mailbox, parked his car and walked through knee-deep snow to help Malvern tote the smaller children out to the plowed county road to take them to Sunday School. Malvern carried Reggie; and Ronald put Annie on his shoulders, dressed as she was in a full snowpants suit. Once they were at church, the two men sang in the quartet while Ron also accompanied on his guitar.

Annie adored Ronald Foerster. Everyone loved him for he was a good, kind, and talented young man.

He was handsome with brown hair and trim frame. His eyes seemed brown because of the spiritual depth in them. Annie puzzled as to what color they really were, but they reminded her of stories about Jesus, for they were totally without malice, and patient.

*

Again, summertime was in full swing, and the Cumming's cousins were up from Nebraska once more. All the kids were bound and determined that this would be the summer during which Malvern's buried treasure would reveal itself, providing they weren't too lazy to dig it up.

Annie and Cherry were at the age when deviling the boys was great fun. Of course, the pranks they pulled were never too off the wall, because both of them were tenderhearted and didn't want to actually hurt Jan, Reginald nor Sammy's feelings, let alone their bodies. Both sensitivities and bodies were to be cherished, Malvern and Daisy had taught the brood.

"You see, the Bible says that our bodies are temples of His Holy Spirit, which is omnipresent, meaning everywhere all at once. That spirit dwells within each of us, in our hearts. We must show respect by taking good care of his temples, don't you agree?"

In assent, all the kids' heads bobbed up and down like buoys on water during a stiff wind.

Marla, being older, had more grown-up things to do than play silly games. Summer band kept her busy at school, until she left to be a counselor and lifeguard at Bible Camp.

*

There was excitement afoot. Everyone thought Daisy had just put on weight from all the good ice cream and food she had been making. But one day around the supper table, a glowing Malvern announced that a new baby would be making his or her debut. He then took the Bible, turned to the book of Psalms and read that blessed was the man whose children were as numerous as arrows in the quiver of an archer. Annie felt wonderful when he said, "Kids are a direct blessing of the Lord!" With great emotion Malvern told how much he and Mother loved them, including cousins Sammy and Cherry. Now, he continued, a new blessing was to arrive after Christmas in approximately six months.

"Praise the Lord for you wonderful children, and this new baby He is sending,"

Mr. Cummings smilingly exalted.

Daisy glowed, and said that they had decided to name the baby with a Hebrew name which meant "happy," providing it was a boy, for not only were they happy when she discovered that a child was on the way, but the unborn baby was, too, for it felt as if he were clapping his little hands inside her tummy every now and then.

"Do you need gas pills?" Annie asked.

Sammy, Cherry, Marla and Jan started laughing and Reginald looked embarrassed. Daisy and Malvern just grinned.

Annie was excited, and couldn't quite comprehend it all. She was full of anticipation.

The kids were going to town with Cherry and Sammy to spend the night at Grandpa and Grandma Illy's house! To stay there was a treat! For in each bedroom was a genuine featherbed which Grandmother and her sisters had sewn together when they were teenagers. To jump into bed and land on billows of soft, fluffy puff was like experiencing heaven. The kids sitting around the supper table couldn't imagine anything that felt better as they plied their knives and forks from plates to mouths and back again.

"Annie, put the food back on your plate and cut it into three pieces. You mustn't take such big bites," Mama directed.

"Yes, Mama," Annie blushed.

"You must be a lady," Daisy reiterated the teaching she had received as a child.

While everyone was eating, hard, blue eyes watched furtively from outside the house through the kitchen window which gave a clear view of the dining room table.

After dinner as Annie skipped past the kitchen porch to hide while playing kick-the-can with everyone, she thought she heard a strange, low laugh from behind the lilac bush. Looking over her shoulder, she saw nothing and soon it was forgotten.

"Run, run, Annie!" Jan shouted as she furiously pumped her eight year old legs as fast as she could to get to the empty honey can on home plate. "Kick the can before Sammy tags you!"

“Ha! Ha! Ha! I’m going to get you!” Sammy laughed as he thumped her back; “You’re it!” he shouted just as she sent the can flying with a swift kick.

“Ha, ha to you, too!” she chortled, “I kicked it before you touched me!”

Now the sneaky eyes watched from the dark interior of the pump house. More and more they liked the littlest blond girl. ‘The other one could probably punch my lights out,’ he silently ascertained, sizing up eleven-year-old Cherry who occasionally whacked her bro a good one on the arm.

“Hey, kids,” Malvern called quietly as he came out the screen door on the east porch. “Anyone want to go to Grandma Illy’s house?”

“I do!” Jan, Reggie, Sammy, Cherry and Annie chorused.

“Get your swim suits. Grandpa Illy is going to take you swimming at Leaf Lakes. Hurry now.” He laughed contentedly watching them all scamper for the house in search of water gear.

Malvern crossed the grass and went into the pump house to look for a screwdriver. A shadowy figure shrank against the brick wall, fading into the absence of light next to the fireplace chimney and held his breath.

Malvern picked up the tool, and singing, "Oh what a beautiful morning, oh what a beautiful day" in his mellow voice, walked to the car. Shortly, off to Grandma and Gramps they all went.

Of course, the big announcement was: "Mama is going to have a baby."

"Is that right?" they asked the children.

"Oh, yes! And, guess what else; I never saw Daddy smile so much. He was happy and read to us out of the Bible where it says we are arrows in his quiver," Annie added importantly.

"Oh?" Grandpa asked, choking on a cookie. Grandma tried not to laugh.

"I think that is just a comparison, Annie," Cherry explained. "Do you know what a quiver is?"

"No," Annie answered. "It must be his chin. I've seen chins quiver before people cry."

"Stupid!" Sammy said. "A quiver is a bag full of arrows on a bowman's back!"

"YOU'RE stupid!" said Reggie, defending his little sister. "It's not a bowman - it's an ARCHER!"

"All I know is that daddies get really happy when Mamas are going to have babies!" Annie retorted. Annie stuck her impudent face up into Sammy's. "So! Am I an arrow?" She felt the top of her head to see if it had suddenly become pointed.

*

The next morning Grandmother's telephone rang at five after nine. It was Mother asking that Annie ride home on her bicycle which had been left at the Illy's two days earlier.

"Would you like to go with Daddy and me to the dentist, dear?" she asked her daughter.

"Will he make me a turtle after he looks at my teeth?" Annie asked. The tooth doctor always made ceramic toys on a tiny machine immediately after each child survived a turn in the chair.

"I am sure he will," Daisy replied.

"Goodie! May Cherry come along?"

"If she wishes to come, she may, dear."

"How will she get to our house if I ride the bike home?"

"Daddy will pick her up on his way through town before we leave. He's at the West Farm this morning," Daisy concluded the phone call. "Goodbye, dear. Leave Grandma's as soon as you've had your breakfast."

"I've already eaten, Mama," Annie confided. "I can start out right now. Cherry is still asleep and Grandma will tell her about it when she wakes up."

"Okay, dear. I will look for you to be home in fifteen minutes. Do be careful and ride at the edge of the road on the shoulder. I'll be praying for you as you pedal the mile home. It's so pretty outdoors, you will enjoy it today." Her mom hung up the telephone.

Putting the receiver into the cradle, Annie announced all her news and that she must go home pronto to get ready to go to the appointment.

Grandma walked her to the garage by the garden where Annie's red bicycle had been safely stored. With a hug and a kiss Annie was off on her bike.

Eyes had been watching from across the street and down the block unbeknown to Grandma and her little Annie. Watching curly yellow hair flying in the breeze as the girl peddled toward the cemetery at the edge of town, dark purpose made them glitter.

Quietly the man got into his car and waited to start the engine until Annie was out of sight. Waiting for the child's grandmother to enter her house, he started the motor, backed out of his driveway and proceeded toward the Cummings farm, following a different avenue which would not take him past the Illy's.

"She should be near the creek on the state highway by the time I catch up to her," he said to his imaginary pal who went with him everywhere. "How do I know, you ask?" he chuckled. "I've watched her go from her grandparent's house before. For years now I've seen her and her little neighbor walk home from school, too. They do that sometimes instead of riding the school bus." He laughed long and low, steering the black car onto the tar road. Gaining a little speed, he was soon in sight of Annie who was pumping away, hair and sweater flowing in the breeze. Rolling his window down, he could hear snatches of the song, "Yes, Jesus loves me, Yes, Jesus loves me, Yes, Jesus loves me, the Bible tells me so."

Annie stood up on the pedals and pumped to ascend a hill after she crossed the creek bridge. The world was bright with dew which still adorned the tall grasses in the highway ditches. Little purple violets were nestled like amethystine nuggets between verdant blades and leaves. She saw her favorite springtime flowers in the marsh bogs beside the stream, and wanted to get off her bike to go pick a fist full for her mother.

"Yellow cowslips are so bright and pretty, just like sunshine," she said aloud.

Starting to slow her bike, suddenly the memory of her mother's voice came to her saying, "I will look for you to be home in fifteen minutes." Annie's heart sank. She knew that if she lollygagged to pick flowers, she would be home later than that, and then Mama would not like the flowers very much.

"After all, 'obedience is better than sacrifice.' I guess the cowslips are the sacrifice because I can't pick any for Mama." The part of her thought which she understood the most was the obedience to her mother's timetable and her own keen disappointment.

When she stopped to catch her breath at the top of the hill, she heard a car behind her. It sounded strange, as if it was going in low gear. She knew about gears. Low ones in her dad's tractor were for pulling and poking along. Turning around, she was startled to see a black car coming slowly toward her on the edge of the road instead of staying on the blacktop.

"What's he doing?" she wondered in a sudden grip of fear. She could see a smallish man behind the wheel. He didn't look nice and was coming straight at her! There was a big grin on his round, flat face and he didn't have much hair. She had seen him before when he'd been hanging around the school yard to watch the kids play during recess. The teacher hadn't been there. Since it was such a small town and everyone so friendly, none of the girls gave the skinny little man a second thought. People in town and in the community were so good.

But this fellow's azure eyes had never

seemed quite right. There was an odd look in them. And the kids often had wondered why he was never at work like their own dads.

Now, Annie's heart turned over with fear. Her mouth felt dry. The car got closer and closer. Suddenly she realized that he was not going to stop. He was not going to turn to avoid hitting her! She heard the same low laugh of two nights earlier when playing kick-the-can.

"I did hear someone," she wheeled around jumping harder onto the pedals and taking off as fast as she could. "It was him!"

Within seconds her bike was flying over the ditch edge down into a sand and gravel pit. 'His car can't follow me here,' she thought. Zooming toward a pile of gravel as tall as a one story building, the bike fell, spilling her onto her knees and hands. Too scared to scream or cry, she scrambled up, bloody knees soaking through torn overalls. Running as fast as her legs could go, she looked back to see where the car was. It had stopped on the edge of the road above the spot where she had fled with her bike. She hid behind yet another mountain of gravel, wedging her body into a depression which had been made by the teeth and bucket of a machine.

"Dear Jesus," she desperately prayed inside of herself, "Please don't let him find me! Oh, please, dear Jesus. Send Daddy to save me!" She held her breath for fear the man would hear her. She just KNEW that he could hear her heart beating. It seemed to be shaking her whole body.

Footsteps sounded on the gravel, crunching slowly, first one then another. Suddenly, it was quiet. A meadowlark trilled in the field on the hill behind Annie. She remembered in a flash the first time she had ever heard the bird's distinctly melodious song. She had been riding with Daddy and Marla in the front seat of the DeSoto on the way to church the day of the thumb sucking discussion.

"If only Daddy were here now!" tears started oozing silently down her round cheeks. She wiped them out of her eyes willing them to stop. She HAD to be quiet, or the man would hear her.

"I mustn't cry. I mustn't cry! I'll wait and cry later after God sends Daddy to rescue me!" she thought to herself.

Her heart stopped. She heard the footsteps starting up again, coming slowly but surely, closer and closer...scraping when they'd stop as the antagonizer peered around one pile of gravel, and then another.

"Sing, 'Jesus Loves Me,' sweetheart," a man's quiet voice called. "I thought that was such a pretty song. Sing it for me again," he coaxed into the still morning air.

The meadowlark trilled again as if to warn the little girl to stay still.

The man laughed, long and low, at the sound.

"Not you, bird!" he raved. "I want Goldilocks to sing it for me, and then I will find her." Suddenly the footsteps stopped again.

Annie could feel him near. She could hardly breathe. The hair on her arms stood up encased in newly formed goose bumps of fear. She suddenly was ice cold. "Oh, Jesus PLEASE send Daddy!" she prayed in her heart.

The scrunching of pebbles started up again as two brown boots came around her gravel pile. She dropped farther down into the hole quietly, squeezing her eyes shut as her left foot painfully slipped between two sharp rocks. Dislodged pebbles bounced to the bottom of the crevice, breaking the pregnant silence.

The man started laughing quietly. Annie could hear the sinister sound and buried her fingers into the gravelly wall of the pit trying not to slip down farther. Opening her eyes, she saw the toes of shoes, and pants cuffs right in front of her.

"How does he not SEE me?" she frantically wondered. She tried to scream, but no sound would come, for it was as if an angel had touched her vocal chords, whispering, "Be still."

A horn started honking up on the highway. Honking! Honking! Honking! It would not stop blaring. She heard, "Annie! Annie! Annie! Where are you?" A car door slammed shut, Annie could hear feet pounding down the gravel filled ditch, half sliding, half running, sending rocks and pebbles spraying in all directions.

Her optics wide as saucers, she saw the stalker's shoes turn around, dragging slowly. Annie froze.

"It's DADDY! It's DADDY!" her mind wildly screamed at her. But the brown shoes wouldn't go away. Pulling her head down like a turtle, she was too afraid to answer her father. Then, she heard the feet near her turn again.

They took a few steps closer, and closer toward her hiding place.

"Oh, Jesus! Let Daddy FIND me!" she almost choked aloud in fear. Suddenly Annie realized she had to use the bathroom. "Oh, dear Jesus, PLEASE don't let me wet my pants!" Tears started down her dusty cheeks in earnest. Sweat was stinging her eyes, but she didn't dare let go of her tenacious hold of the gravel-pit wall.

Nestling her face into the dirt, the terrified girl shoved her mouth against it and bit to make herself stop wanting to cry. "One sob and I'll give myself away!" she panicked. The pain in her feet and legs was almost unbearable.

"Why, Mr. Thwacker! What are you doing here?" her dad's voice, now quiet and friendly, was suddenly very near. "Is that your car stalled up on the road?" Malvern wisely plied the crazed man who stood, mouth agape, peering sideways at the newcomer's straw hat which was shining in the sun.

Mr. Thwacker turned slowly to face Annie's father. Mr. Cummings knew good and well what Thwacker was about! But, a confrontational battle wasn't necessary. Everyone except the village children knew that the man was not mentally fit. Everyone also knew that he fell prey to suggestion very easily if quietly coached. No one knew as to what extent his unfortunate madness might take him some day - and if this was any barometer of things yet to come, it was very sobering indeed!

Malvern wanted no violence. Annie, wherever she was, must be horrified enough without that, he thought. He couldn't see her. But, he had seen her bike sprawled in the gravel.

Malvern felt Annie's presence. It was palpably reaching out to him with terrified longing.

The little girl shivered, too frightened to look over the edge of her shelter.

"Hi, Mal!" the demented stalker greeted the rescuer. "I wanted to check the gravel density. I need a load for my driveway," Mr. Thwacker said.

"I see," Malvern picked the straw fedora off his own head and brushed golden hair in a backward stroke.

"Well, your house is less than a mile away. Why don't you go home and place your order now? Maybe the gravel company can haul it for you before they get too busy today."

Sensing that his little Annie was within sight and sound of his voice, he didn't want her innocence compromised by having to witness a fist fight or worse.

"Yes, that's a good idea," the unsavory man said, much to Malvern's relief. Mr. Thwacker started moving away toward the steep incline of the ditch to get back to his car. Mr. Cummings watched the unfortunate go up the dirt bank, get into his vehicle, make a u-turn and drive off toward town. Mal stood stalk still. He wasn't going to give his little girl's hiding place away – she might need it again some day. He felt that she was inches away, but couldn't see her. Patiently he waited until Thwacker's car went around a curve.

Turning around Malvern called, "Annie, sweetheart, it's Daddy. I know that you are here. I saw your bike tipped over on the gravel. He's gone now. It's safe to come out."

No one answered.

The breeze tickled the blades and whiskers of wheat growing in a nearby field. A meadowlark trilled as if rejoicing that the lost lamb was nearly found. Malvern looked around for footprints, but the crushed rock was too large in size to give the imprint of a light step. “Thank God for these little rocks even though they toppled her bike,” he thought as his eyes searched the ground.

“Annie, darling, where are you? It’s Daddy.”

A movement caught his eye and he saw the top of a little yellow head slowly rising from behind a low mound of gravel only inches away.

“Daddy, I’m THTUCK!” she whispered loudly. Her mind was frightened into the lisp of her babyhood.

With a joyful laugh, Malvern called, “Here I come!” as he lunged forward toward the mop of disheveled hair and the sound of her plea. Rounding the heap of gravel, there she was - clean paths caused by quiet tears were being etched down her dirty face. One leg was wedged between two rocks. She had been a trapped, sitting duck. Easily throwing the rocks aside, her daddy scooped his suddenly sobbing little one into arms which hugged her until the small body stopped shaking. With feet dangling off the ground from his grasp, she cried brokenly, "I KNEW you'd come! I KNEW you'd come!"

Clinging to his neck, her wet, sweaty face smelled like chicken feathers that had just been dunked into a pot of boiling water.

Mal gently lowered Annie to the ground. Squatting down he balanced her in one strong arm and onto his knee.

"How did you know, sweetie?" her daddy gently asked as he wiped her wet face with his big red bandana.

"Because I asked Big Daddy in the sky," a sob tore from her chest, "I asked Jesus to send you."

"You DID? You thought of that when you were so scared?" her father asked incredulously, looking into her upturned face.

"Of COURTH, I did!" she answered somewhat indignantly. "You always TELL us that He hears us and will answer our prayers, and He did! He did!" Her body shook with a new fit of sobbing. Her arms squeezed around his neck so tightly, he thought he'd be strangled.

He took time to be still, hugging back as securely as he could without hurting her little frame. Now was not the time for words, just love.

After her crying calmed into little quick breaths, Malvern prayed softly, aloud, smoothing the damp curls from her brow. "Thank You, dear and sweet Jesus Christ. You were once a child. You knew how Annie felt when being chased and hunted. Thank You for sheltering her in Your arms as she hid in this gravel pit. Thank you for answering her prayers to send me. You got me here just in the nick of time. I thank You. Your love overwhelms me; and that You take care of those who trust You, is surely proved to us this day."

Malvern stood up, holding his girl in his arms. "Come, little one, let's go home to Mama." Climbing up to the Desoto he put Annie on the front seat, got in and drove toward home after putting her bike into the trunk.

As they were driving the rest of the way to the farm, Malvern said, "Yes, Annie. Jesus answers prayer. And, after He answers we must act wisely to protect ourselves." Annie's father grinned widely as she looked up at him. "Next time you want to ride your bicycle home, do you think it would be a good idea to have Marla or Jan along, or one of the other boys? I am sure Mother will agree."

"Yes, Daddy-oh, please-may they? I'd like that," her voice trembled. Sliding across the seat to nestle close, her dad opened one arm to welcome her. "Now Mr. Thwacker can't get me!" Annie said.

Annie could hear the beat of her father's heart as her tousled head laid against his side. A sound familiar to her ever since a babe in arms as he read Bible stories to the family, she became greatly comforted.

That afternoon, while Annie was with her mother at the dentist's office, Malvern went to the local authorities who removed the menace from town to the State Hospital, some distance away, for treatment.

Did Annie receive the turtle pin for being a good patient at the dentist's office? Yes. The next Sunday, she proudly wore it on her favorite green dress. With GREAT gusto, she sang a duet with Trisha in which the lyrics said:

"God answers prayer in the morning, God answers prayer at noon, God answers prayer in the evening, so keep your heart in tune."

Annie remembered the gravel pit experience and Daisy later saying, "When you didn't arrive home on time, I called Daddy at the West Farm. He went to find you. Oh, thank God, he went to look for you right away!" and she had thrown her arms around her little daughter.

"Mommie?" Annie had asked.

"Yes, dear," Daisy wiped her own eyes with a handkerchief.

"I am happy that you told me to come home in fifteen minutes; otherwise I would have stopped to pick cowslips for you."

"Is that right, Annie?" her mother asked.

"Yes. But, when I slowed the bike down to go over to the flowers, I remembered you saying that you would look for me in fifteen minutes. So I thought I'd better obey you instead of bringing a sacrifice."

"A SACRIFICE?" her mom asked. "What do you mean?"

"Well, Daddy always tells us that obedience is better than sacrifice. I suppose the flowers would have been the 'sacrifice'."

Her Dad spoke up, "You would have been the sacrifice," and placed his hand on her head. "Yes, this time you would have been the sacrifice, I'm afraid!"

"How, Daddy?" the child asked.

"Because you obeyed your mother, Annie, you were saved. There was no place for you to hide near the flowers, but there was at the top of the hill. God knew that and hid you there until I could catch the fellow and send him away." Daisy clung to her daughter.

"Where is he now?" Annie trembled at the memory of the sinister man's shoes so close to her face as she crouched in the gravel pit.

"He is far away from here under lock and key where he will be treated for his illness which makes him prey upon children," her father comfortingly said.

"But even though this happened, we must pray for him, that God will heal his sick mind, and cause him to do good things. We must forgive him, but God expects us to make sure that he's in a safe place where he will be unable to hurt anyone or frighten them ever again!"

Annie had never seen her papa angry before, but he sure was mad now! Although his voice remained calm and quiet, his eyes were full of lightening.

Malvern gathered everyone together that evening, including Sammy and Cherry. Annie's special friend Ronald, had come immediately to console her by playing his guitar.

Malvern read comforting words from the Bible and prayed for everyone, including the stalker, after first asking God to help the latter find his right mind. In so doing, Annie's father taught the family love and forgiveness. He also asked God to teach everyone wisdom to protect one's self.

"Always play and go biking or swimming with each other," he told the children. "Don't strike out alone, and above all, obey your mom and dad. Be sure to tell us when and where you are going! Let us know the time of day when you leave. Had Annie not done just that and obeyed Mama, I wouldn't have found her in a hiding place. There is no such place in which to be concealed where she was tempted to stop and pick flowers!"

Everyone got onto their knees. All the children took turns praying aloud, elbows resting on overstuffed chairs and davenport in the pale orchid living room. Rising to sit on the cushions trimmed with silken swags, Annie listened to the crystals on the red silk lamp tinkling melodiously as the summer breeze played gently through the house.

Ronald played his guitar and sang while Mama accompanied him on the electric Evestaff pianette.

Annie's terrified soul found peace.

Ronald stopped singing and said, "Well, I must go home now. I have to get up early and help Dad milk the cows." As he put the guitar into its case, he smiled and looked at Annie. "Some sweet day, I hope God will give me a little girl just like you!"

"May I come to the wedding first?" Annie asked.

As everyone laughed, he said, "You surely may, as soon as I find a bride!" Tickling her under the chin as he rose to put on a coat, he winked, said his good-byes and was out the door.

That night Annie dreamed of sliding into a pit where a grizzly was baring its teeth in welcome, rearing on its hind legs to get her. A bloodcurdling scream rent the night.

Light flooded the hall outside Annie and Marla's bedroom as their father dashed upstairs to them.

"Annie, Annie," he gently gathered her against his shoulder. "It's all right, child. It's all right. You're safe in your own bed with Marla."

"Oh, Daddy! He's so big and wild!"

"Who, darling?" he gathered her pajama'd form onto his lap. Marla patted her little sister's knees after rolling over to help.

"The bear! The bear! It's always the bear at the bottom of the pit!" She shook and nestled closer to her father's shirt.

"And where are you in the dream?" he gently asked.

"I always am sliding down the side of the pit. It's like an ice cream cone before the ice cream is put in." She looked helplessly at his strong face.

"You know that there isn't really a bear in here, I think?" he wondered aloud.

"Not now, there isn't, but when I'm

sleeping there is." She clung to him. "Please make it go away. He'll come back in the dark, Daddy; and the Russians."

Malvern's eyebrows shot up in surprise but he said, "Would you like it if I leave the light on in the hall tonight?" Then, "And, what's this about the Russians?"

"Yes, then I can see him coming and wake Marla up to get you," she rubbed her eyes; "radio said Russians want war."

Malvern started singing a song, "What a Friend We Have in Jesus." Soon he was tucking a sleeping Annie under the covers, and with a smile at Marla, went back to Daisy in the master bedroom downstairs. He left the light on as promised, even though hundreds of tiny night insects came through the screen to make a whirling carousel around its frosted globe. By morning they lay motionless on the carpeted floor beneath the scene of their nighttime ecstasy. The hot light had sent them into happy bug-heaven where all good little bugs go when they die.

As Annie slept, she dreamed of her friend, Ronald. She found herself praying

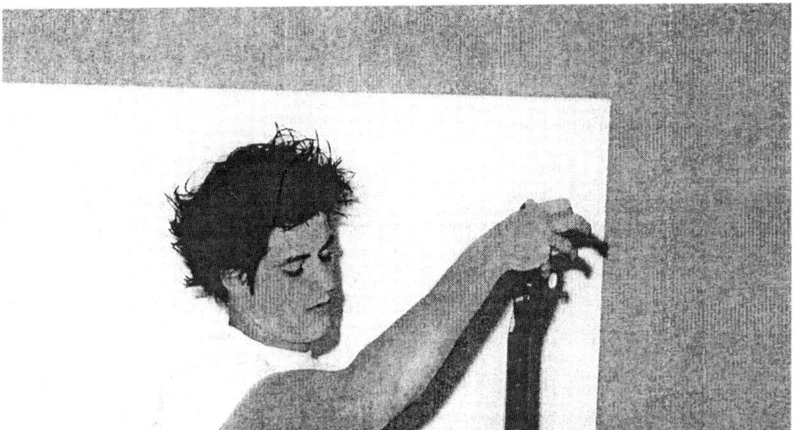

that Jesus would protect him and always let him come to sing to her when she felt bad. Then she dreamed that he was in a white robe which had beautiful wings. Softly they moved in time to the strumming of his guitar as he sang sweet songs of praise to Jesus, who was standing beside him, enjoying the music. Jesus and Ronald seem to be of the same age, and they were obviously great pals, the best of friends, being happy in each other's company.

Annie felt good from the sight. It made her feel as if God would surely answer her prayer of that evening.

"I will have Ronald as my second dad all my life," she murmured in her sleep. A smile broke across her face, and she slept soundly until the sun rose over the eastern hill beyond the bedroom windows.

At breakfast, Mal and Daisy calmed Annie's fears about the post war newscast she had heard. True, in their town near the Canadian border, enemy aircraft vigils from the City Hall tower were kept around the clock, one citizen at a time. "But, if we pray, God will protect our nation and keep it safe," her Daddy assured her. "No planes will be seen from City Hall; for in the Bible, God said He would spare a city if there could be found one righteous man. I know many such men around here, dear, who love Him and live right. He will protect us, too."

Chapter 4

Arsenic and Old Jeans

Marla was practicing her piano lesson. “Hall of the Mountain King”, by Edvard Greig, filled the house with exquisite sounds. The Evestaff instrument was a copy of that which had been given to Princesses Elizabeth and Margaret of England. The unusual piano was a gift to Daisy and the family in order for Marla, especially, to express her musical talents. She proved to be an avid learner and player whose execution was done accurately and with feeling. Marla loved to practice, which Annie did not. The latter would rather run outside to play with the boys; or to play fairy princess under the tall elms which ringed the lawn;

or to pretend she was Lily Pons, prima ballerina, floating in dance from one end of the two acre lawn to the other as strains of Handel, Vivaldi, Hayden and Tchaikovsky wafted their way from the radio. Cranking up the sound full bore, the open windows of the house were great conduits of music. But, when the rendition of Grieg started pumping out butterflies and trolls of his beloved Norwegian mountains, the floating dancer would suddenly be on all fours, scaring her brothers, Sammy or Cherry from behind trees as the kids lounged on cotton blankets in the shade, eating through bags of Grandma's doughnut holes while reading comic books or Look and Life magazines.

"Oh! Annie you pest," they'd yell, giving chase midst shouts of laugher. Annie would hide, wriggling out of her sister's confining skirt and mother's lace mantilla, earrings and necklaces, revealing jeans and blouse. Shoving the jewelry into her pockets, she faced a red-faced Sammy who came around the corner of the pump house, followed by her two brothers.

"After that performance of yours, we'd better do something normal," Sammy announced. "Let's climb the ladder beside the garage so we can jump onto the swing. We filled the sack at the end of the rope with fresh cattail down this morning."

"Yeah! Let's!" everyone agreed.

"Well, we're supposed to take water out to the turkeys as soon as the tank gets full," Jan said.

"Yeh, I know," Sammy said. "But, it isn't full yet, is it?"

"I'll go see," Jan answered, and started across the yard to the water tank which was mounted on four wheels. A black hose was curled up from the back end, with the spout resting in a hook until such time as the boys needed to lower it into the water troughs out in the alfalfa fields where several flocks, totalling 11,000 birds, were ranging.

"I'll help you," Sammy good-naturedly volunteered, and went alongside his taller cousin.

Jan walked over to the green hose which was filling the tank from the water spigot in the long brooder house, while Sammy went the other direction to the back of the tank. He had suddenly developed a thirst.

Taking the black hose off its hook, Sammy lowered it until water started flowing from the tank. Bending over, he drank and drank.

"Boy! This tastes good, Jan. Do you want some?" Sammy wiped his mouth with the back of his hand.

Jan looked up from the top of the tank, where he had climbed in order to check the depth of the water with a long stick.

"Sammy! We're not supposed to drink from the black hose. Dad puts de-wormer medicine in the tank for the turkeys sometimes. It's arsenic! It's poison!" Jan jumped down and ran to his cousin, taking the offending hose from him, and hooking it back onto the side of the water tank.

"Sammy, are you alright?"

Sammy had suddenly paled and was

looking green around the gills.

"Sure. I'm alright. It tasted good," he answered.

"Well, we'd better go tell Mom right away. I know that Dad was going to put arsenic into the tank today. Maybe he hasn't added it yet. Come on, we'd better hurry."

The boys started running for the house, stopping to watch Annie climb the ladder as they passed by. It rested against the sack tied to the rope behind her, she got to the top rung. Turning around, she called to the boys, "Watch me!" and let the bag go. Upon its return, Annie jumped off the eighth rung, catching the rope with her hands while clamping her legs around the top of the bag for a perfectly thrilling ride beneath the benevolent elm tree branch. "I love it!" she called to the onlookers.

"Yes? Well you shouldn't go so high on the ladder, Annie. What if you missed?" Jan called to her.

"You do it and you don't miss!" Annie yelled back as the bag brought her close to him and Sammy, then took her beyond reach, back and forth, back and forth.

"Well, we're older," Jan solemnly replied.

"Does that make you smarter?" Annie plaintively answered as her feet came close to the boys' heads.

"Not smarter, moppet, just more accurate, I think," he replied. "Anyway, you've been cross-eyed lately and Mama is going to take you to the eye-doctor to get glasses tomorrow. You don't want to add a crack to your head, do you?"

"No."

"Well then, until your eyesight is better, maybe you should go up to the sixth rung, not the eighth. Okay?"

"If you say so," Annie grinned. "But, a big sweep is more fun!"

"You're right about that!" Jan tweaked her red shoe as it flew past his waist.

"Come on, Sammy, let's go find Mom." The boys walked into the house.

Jan suddenly emerged from the house

faster than he had entered. He was in a dead run, the door slamming behind him. (NO ONE was allowed to let doors bang in the Cumming's house.)

"What's the matter, Jan?" Annie jumped off the bag and ran after him.

"Stay back, Annie. I have to run find Dad!" Jan jumped on a tractor and fired it up. Pushing the stick forward, the big beast snorted to life. The big wheels started rolling. Hazy fumes poured out of the tall stack on its strange body. "Go to Mama, Annie!" Jan ordered in no uncertain terms.

Annie went to Mama!

"Yes," Daisy was saying into the telephone. "Malvern will be here in just a few minutes. We'll take Sammy to the hospital to have his stomach pumped." She listened awhile. "Okay, don't worry. No, I don't think you'll have to come up. It would take twelve hours for you to get here. It's a long drive." She listened more.

"I'll call you in an hour from the hospital."

Just then, Annie saw Grandpa Illy's

car coming up the driveway. She ran out to him.

"Grandpa, what's wrong?" she anxiously asked.

"Sammy drank arsenic out of the turkey tank," Mr. Illy replied.

"What's arsenic?" Annie wanted to know.

"It's poison, which, when used sparingly on fowl, benefits them rather than kills. But, for humans it's not good."

Annie felt tears well into her eyes. Sammy was going to die! Her Sammy was going to die!

"Oh, Grandpa! Sammy isn't going to die, is he?" She looked past Grandpa to Grandma, who was already out of the car and walking to the house.

"Not if we get him straight to the hospital," Grandpa answered.

Grandma helped get queasy Sammy off a chair. Daisy and Mrs. Illy supported him between them, even though the boy, mightily embarrassed said, "I don't feel bad. I can walk by myself."

Annie looked on helplessly, but prayed silently with all her might. God had saved her from the bad man; now she just knew he'd save her cousin from dying!

She adored the ground on which her cousin walked, and didn't want him to be taken out of her sight. She felt that if they took him away, she'd never see him again. To make matters worse, she didn't know for sure whether or not he was what her church called 'saved.' One had to be saved to go to heaven, they said.

Sometimes Sammy told her naughty jokes that were cute, but that made her think of things which caused her cheeks to burn. But, he was never filthy mouthed like some of the hired men when they didn't know any of the kids were within hearing distance. Sammy sometimes just said things that were frowned upon in the presence of ladies.

So, she didn't know if Sammy was ready to meet his Maker or not! Daddy always said that sweet and bitter water couldn't come from the same well.

Kind words would come from the wellspring of one's heart, or naughty and bitter. If they were good and inoffensive to others, it would be caused by the purity of the Christ within us, he'd say. If words were the opposite, it would not be His Spirit controlling the tongue. "And people's hearts and minds are supposed to be the places where God lives. We are his temples," he'd always add.

"Dear Jesus, please save Sammy before he dies," Annie brushed the tears from her cheeks. "Better yet, please don't let him die. You don't need him but we do! He makes us laugh!"

The tractor came racing around the corner of the machine shed from the north field. Malvern's yellow curls (or what was left of them, for he had slowly been losing his hair) were blowing in the wind. Jan was riding on the fender of the tractor beside his father.

Pulling the tractor to a halt, Mal jumped down and ran to Grandpa Illy's car. By that time Sammy was in the back seat beside Mrs. Illy.

"Sammy, are you still able to stay awake?" he asked.

"Yes, Uncle Malvern," he nodded tiredly.

"How do you feel?" his uncle probed.

"Well, I'm a little sleepy is all."

"Would you mind if we all prayed a short prayer before we go twenty miles to the hospital?" Malvern asked.

"No, I won't mind. That would be nice," Sammy mumbled foggily.

"Hurry up, Malvern! He might die by the time you finish!" Daisy urged. Everyone including Sammy got tickled. Malvern plopped a gentle hand on Sammy's shoulder through the open window. Raising his other hand to heaven, he quietly beseeched the Lord to slow the effects of the arsenic until it could be safely purged from Sammy's body. Reaching in further, Malvern gave Sammy a big hug.

By that time, Sammy's head fell onto Grandma's shoulder and she steadied him in her arm, patting his cheek.

"I'll follow you in our car," Mal said to Grandpa as he walked away, guiding his pregnant wife toward their own vehicle. Helping Daisy in, he shut the door, rushing around to the driver's side calling, "Jan, thanks for coming to get me! Please take Annie and Reg with you inside. If you kids want ice cream, go ahead. Read or play games while we're gone. I'd feel better knowing that all of you are in the house with Marla and Cherry until we get back. Of course, you can swing or lie in the shade of the trees in the yard. It's such a pretty day. But don't get separated!"

With that, his foot tromped the accelerator, Daisy's head jerked backward as they raced out of the dusty driveway to catch up with Mr. Illy's blue Cadillac.

A couple of hours later, a telephone call came for the anxious kids .

"Sammy, Sammy!" Annie prayed, holding her breath. She just KNEW that he had died! She felt sick to her stomach. It felt as if something had cracked inside the middle of her chest. Tears welled unbidden and started down her cheeks.

"Okay. I will," Jan said. "Okay, Dad. Thanks." He hung up the telephone onto the wall receiver.

The five children were so quiet they could hear the birch leaves rustling outside through the open living room door. Fragrant summer breezes hit their noses as they sat, books in hand. Cherry's big eyes asked, 'Well?' as she looked at Jan, expectantly hoping for the best. Annie's blouse was getting soaked from silent tears which had been dripping off her face. She loved Sammy so much it hurt!

Jan walked over to Annie, handing her a red bandana from his hip pocket. "Here, Annie," he said, "you can dry your tears now. If you keep on crying, you won't be able to go to the bathroom anymore because all the water is coming out of your eyes!"

All the kids laughed except Annie. But, she grinned through the snot and tears.

"Do you mean..." she looked trustingly up at him. She choked. Jan thumped her on the back, took the hankie from her grubby little paw and wiped her nose.

"Blow!" he commanded.

She blew.

"Is Sammy okay?" Cherry asked in her forthright manner. "That brother of mine!"

"Yah! Speak up! Is he ALIVE?" Reginald tremulously swallowed tears.

"Well, Jan?" Cherry hardly dared ask again.

Marla sat, quietly worrying.

"What? What news?" Annie tugged on Jan's wrist, pulling his hand and the handkerchief down from her face.

"He's ALIVE!" Jan said with quiet fervor. Like his dad, he never raised his voice, but was intense just the same. He coughed and then wiped his own nose. "I must have caught a cold," he excused his teary eyes and runny nostrils.

"HOORAY!" everyone chorused.

"Hot diggety!" Annie and Cherry shouted as they jumped up, swinging each other around in circles clear out the front door midst shrieks of laughter.

Reginald sat with his head down, slowly gulping tears of thanksgiving to God which welled from his sensitive soul. He took his thick glasses off, and wiped them on his grubby shirt. A little mud developed on the lenses. He didn't mind. Sammy was alive and going to be fine!

Marla smiled her mild, beautiful way, and asked if anyone would like root beer floats.

"Yes!" they all said. Jan said, "Is there anything else to eat besides?"

"Did I hear the word 'floats'?" Cherry asked as she and Annie came back indoors.

"I'm not hungry," Reginald said solemnly and went upstairs.

"It's only four o'clock. We'll have floats and wait for everyone to come home from the hospital. I'll make supper, and if they aren't here by six o'clock, we'll keep theirs warm in the oven and go ahead and eat," Marla said. She was so grown up already and only eleven years old!

"Now, that's a plan!" Cherry said.

"Here, let me help you. Where's the ice cream?" Cherry was Jan's age - all of nine.

"Save some for Sammy!" Annie cried. "he will be hungry when he gets back. They pumped his stomach empty and it's pretty big, you know!"

Everyone laughed.

"He will be in the hospital all night, Annie," Jan said. "They want to keep an eye on him to make sure he will get well."

"Please, will you save him some of mine, anyway?" Annie teared up again. "He liketh root beer floaths." She had started to lisp again.

She slipped out the door and ran to her favorite hiding place in the sweet-smelling haymow, threw herself face down on the hay, buried her face in her arms, and cried.

And cried.

And cried.

*

It was already dark by the time Malvern found Annie in the hay lying fast asleep, tear-stained face peacefully buried on her arm. Everyone had been looking for her for hours, but this time no one scolded her, for they knew that her little heart had been comforted by God's mercy and tender goodness which had been bestowed upon her dearly beloved cousin.

When Sammy was safely home, Annie told her mother, "I have a secret."

"What's that darling?"

"Well, when Sammy drank poison, I thought he'd die. So I decided that when I get big, I'll marry Sammy to keep him safe. You see, sometimes he does stupid things. But, he doesn't mean to."

Daisy brushed her hair thoughtfully, sitting at the vanity. She put the brush down, motioned Annie to come into her arms, and tilting the little face up to her gentle gaze said, "You can't marry Sammy, darling. He's your first cousin."

Annie felt like her future was over! "But why does that matter, Mama?"

"Because you both have the same kind of blood. If you marry each other, your children will either be geniuses or idiots."

Annie thought that one over for a good four years until Health class, in seventh grade, enlightened her.

*

Chapter 5

Angel Wings and Guitars

A few weeks later, the stalker squinted up at the judge.

"Yes, I'll stay away from her, your honor," Mr. Thwacker said.

"And, you will no longer stand beside the playground at school during the childrens' recess periods, nor before nor after school when they are going to and fro?" the judge pressed for another answer.

"That's right, your honor! That's right. I've learned a good lesson, I have." He shook his head up and down.

"Well, then, you may be released into the custody of your aging mother and father. But if you even come close to making a nuisance of yourself in that community, you will be right back in the Hill! Do I make myself clear?"

"Yes, your judgeship ... er ... honor. Yes."

"Okay, then Mrs. Thwacker. You may take your son home."

A tired elderly woman looked up worriedly at the judge.

The gavel was smacked onto its wooden pad and a firm, "Court dismissed!" sounded throughout the high-ceilinged room. Chairs scraped as attorneys, psychiatrists, judge and clients got up to leave.

The stalker was on the loose again.

*

Ronald Foerster was such a joy to everyone at the little white Baptist church. Annie felt safe with him around, and she could trustingly put her hand in his if she needed help at Sunday School picnics when climbing up lake banks, or wading barefoot on rocky shorelines; or getting in line at the picnic table which the good ladies of the church had filled to overflowing with chicken, potato salad, coleslaw, fruit Jell-O heaped with whipped cream, rich chocolate cakes with boiled, smooth, fudge frosting; angel foods made with a whisk from fresh egg whites, their sister sponge cakes made from the yokes of the same eggs. Lemonade by the milk cans full was plentiful and lasted the entire days of such affairs. And always, Ronald, with his sweet singing as he played acoustical guitar, was a treat in itself.

"Come on, Annie, let's go down to the point to play games. Maybe you will win a prize or two," Ronald encouraged the reluctant child at a Sunday School picnic one day.

Annie blushed because she didn't want to exhibit at games in front of all the church. She hated the competitions unless she could just watch. Always, she battled against the dreaded shyness which pained her to the very core when having to do something unfamiliar in front of others. Singing with Trish didn't bother her because she was secure in her friend's love and acceptance, and in the fact that Trish's mom loved her, too. She practically lived at their house when Daisy was sick in bed, which was most of every weekend and many school days. She even had a place at the Welland's table, and sat there automatically at meal times. She and Trish helped do the dishes, wiping the sink afterward until it sparkled like snow, for that pleased Mrs. Welland.

Now, to put herself forward in competition against a bunch of scrambling bodies somehow hurt her dignity. It felt like a threat of some kind. Something didn't seem right about herself winning a prize if the other kids didn't get one, too. Some of the girls and boys never won at anything in sports. Some of them were poor, and she wanted them to win the toys, not herself.

Her daddy, mom and grandparents gave her everything. She liked to share and give things away. Her parents had to tactfully help her to stop it.

"Come on, sweet pea," Ronald took her hand, calling to Malvern who came to walk with them. Walking between the two, hand-in-hand, the three proceeded toward the play field.

"I guess there is going to be a tug-of-war," Malvern joyfully said. He was strong as an ox, and loved to be singled out to join in the game of brute strength.

"Yes, that's what I heard!" Ronald laughed. "I'd rather play my guitar."

"Well, you're good at three-legged racing, too," Malvern complimented his friend. "You've good coordination. Want to be my partner?"

Annie squinted against the sun to look up at them - first one, and then the other. They both seemed so tall. Their heads had clouds floating above them.

"Yes, why not! I'd like that," Ronald affirmed.

"Maybe if we sing while we run, we won't get out of step and fall down," Mal laughed.

"We could sing 'The old grey mare, she ain't what she used to be, ain't what she used to be, ain't what she used to be.' That goes at a good clip," Ron said.

Annie wondered why the song said 'ain't' when Mama said there was no such word.

"Mama won't like that song," Annie observed.

"Why not, squirt?" Mal asked.

"She won't let us say ain't." Annie sneezed from squinting up through the sunlight at her dad's tanned face.

Malvern handed her his white, Sunday handkerchief. It smelled nice and clean like bluing, a delicate scent which she loved so well.

Grandma Illy used the same kind of blue bar, shaving it into the washing machine water to make white clothes whiter.

"Thank you, Daddy," Annie sneezed again into the hanky.

"That's true, Annie, but the song is a Folk song, and its lyrics are accepted because part of our populace says 'ain't.' He smiled down at her as she handed the handkerchief back.

"May I say 'ain't' like Molly does?"

"No, darling. You may not."

"What's wrong with Molly?"

"Nothing's wrong with Molly, dear! You just may not say 'ain't.' We prefer another form of speech." He bent down and gave his little girl a squeeze.

"Okay, Daddy." To please him was all the reason she needed not to use the offending word.

The games started. Annie's age group lined up for the three-legged dash. Thank God, Trish had grabbed her to secure a partner for the gunny sack race!

"Now I can race with confoundedness!" Annie exclaimed in joy.

Trisha started to laugh. "Not confoundedness, Annie! CONFIDENCE!" She laughed more. "You and your big words-you are so funny!" She said, "Here, stick your foot in the poke with mine," and held up the other half of a half-full-of-half-Trish brown cloth bag.

Annie lifted her leg and started to aim for the hole. Suddenly she lost her balance, her foot got stuck in the top of the bag. She couldn't get her foot back out, and they landed in a heap on the grass.

Trish laughed and laughed, pulling Annie up once she got on her own feet again. Annie was blushing furiously because she saw Jan looking painfully at her; Reggie grinning through his lenses; and Brysie's eyes dancing behind a polite smile. She whirled around so as not to see them, thinking she was glad Sammy had gone fishing with Grandpa. If her cousin had seen her fall, he would have laughed and teased her for the rest of her entire life!

"Here, you stick your leg in first, Annie," Trish offered. Annie put her foot into the lowered burlap bag. Trish pulled it up a little and put her left foot in, stepping on a hidden gopher mound.

Down they went again! This time

Trish almost howled with laughter. Annie's face became more crimson. Everyone was chuckling quietly. She wished the ground would do her a favor – open up and swallow her, flush her through a magic tube right into Grandma Illy's arms! She felt herself being lifted up from behind.

"Here, sweetheart, let me help you," the Pastor's wife offered. She lifted Annie, then took Trisha by the hand and pulled her up, too.

"Let's get you two into the sack," the preacher's wife said. She got them ready just in time for the first pop of a cap gun, which signaled that the race was to begin.

"Okay, Annie. When the second shot goes off, start running with your left foot and don't get out of step!" Trish advised.

The gun exploded. People started yelling. Annie's heart pounded as she and Trish matched each other's stride as easily as their voices when they sang duets at church. Faster and faster they lumped along like a three-legged monster, holding the bag up around their waists.

"Hurry, Annie, hurry!" Trish shouted.

Annie hurried.

Suddenly a flash of red and blue whizzed past them. Wernadine, with Roz in her sack, sailed past like a tall ship being chased by pirates. Laughingly falling into a heap, the dashing duo broke through a string Ronald and Mal were holding at the finish line.

"We won! We won!" Wernadine hopped up and down with Roz as they wriggled out of the burlap sack.

Annie flopped down on the ground, pulling Trish after. Shaking the ungainly bag off their skinny little legs, Annie exclaimed, "I'm GLAD they won!"

"So am I," Trish said. "Come on, let's go get a piece of chocolate cake with fudge frosting!"

"But, isn't that for supper?"

"We'll start supper early!" Trisha pulled Annie up, and off they scampered through the crowd toward the picnic tables at the other end of the park. Checkered table cloths of red and white held the booty.

Newspapers were spread over the sweets to keep flies off, and unsavory elements of nature (birds are pretty, but not necessarily a welcome sight perched on tree boughs which shade picnic tables.)

Two grubby little hands stole beneath the loose coverings. Soon, satisfied smacking and licking of fingers could be heard from behind the chokecherry bushes if one listened closely.

*

After supper, Ronald sat at the campfire beside Malvern and Annie, playing his guitar. Favorite choruses were sung by everyone together. Ronald eventually sang a solo by popular demand. His beautiful tenor voice seemed to embrace the night sky, making the stars dazzle in wonder. He then sang a quartet number with Malvern,

Daisy and Ron's sister.

Forty little sets of shoulders snuggly wrapped in jackets and summer blankets basked in the beautiful music and smell of birch logs snapping in the fire. Stars vied for the kids' attention with the fireflies which were showing off their luminescent talents. Sammy couldn't help himself. He just had to snatch at a few to sequester in his grubby pockets. Reggie wrote his own name on his shirt with one unhappy firefly, but then let the poor defrocked insect fly into the night with no guiding light to show the way home. After the songfest was over, the children screeched and laughed as they ran about, vying for the same bugs to put into Kerr jars, securing them with lids into which air holes had been poked. The lanterns were great for lighting the path back to the cars. Minnesota's pine, cottonwood, elm and birch rustled in the light breeze off the lake as the moon tipped water, and foliage with silver.

"I liked how you told us about Jesus making you so happy since you gave your heart to Him, Ronald," Jan said as he walked beside the young singer who wasn't many years his senior.

Ronald smiled.

"And that last song you sang, 'If We Never Meet Again This Side of Heaven,' gave me goose bumps," Annie piped up to add through the darkness. She was walking hand-in-hand between Jan and Ronald, peering up at the singer through the glow of the lightning bug lamp Jan was carrying in his other hand. Ronald's guitar, swinging softly from his shoulder, made a hollowly soft metallic sound as it thump, thump, thumped against his back and slender hip.

"Thank you, Annie. It stirred me tonight, too." Ronald looked down at her, squeezing her little hand in his big one.

They had reached the cars, and along with the rest of their friends and parents, got into their respective DeSotos, Chevies, Fords, Studebakers and Buicks.

"Time to let the fireflies go, Jan and Reg. You, too, Sammy. You can empty your pockets now. The insects have done their work. Now they get to go home and sleep just like you!" Malvern laughed.

A fire shower of bugs suddenly lit the darkness as the kids minded the boss.

Chapter 6

Tragedy

One day a menacing, black sky in the west brought Malvern and the boys in from the fields. Lightning was flickering wickedly in great bolts as if being thrust by Zeus toward the farms all around.

"It's just not safe to be on a tractor in this stuff," Malvern had told Jan, Reggie and Sammy. "Come on, we're going home. Leave the equipment in the field. Help me unhook it from the tractor." He and the boys dismounted and after securing everything, climbed into the enclosed safety of Mal's truck.

Once home, Sammy decided to go into town to the Illy's. ALL the kids decided to go along for the night there, if the storm would hold back long enough for them to grab night clothes and get to the car in one piece. Before the storm broke, the kids and Daisy rode with Malvern to check the turkey flocks which were in the open hay fields, sheltering under immense roosts.

"We need to check them on the range, kids," Malvern exclaimed as a great flash of lightning and resounding crash of thunder made everyone in the car jump. Buckets of wind-lashed rain started pouring from the sky. It came so fast and furiously that it was raining completely sideways instead of vertically.

It was in the nature of turkeys to flock together tightly by the hundreds to seek shelter. Many would suffocate to death if someone didn't wade through their midst, stirring them to provide breathing space.

Watching her strong father and brothers climb out of the car into the driving sheets of rain midst the sudden blackness which was lit only by the car headlight and lightning, made Annie's heart quake with fear. She watched through streaming windows as her dad suddenly sent the boys back to the car.

Annie was sweating from the pressure brought to bear by anxiety.

"Open the door! Open the door!" the soaked boys shouted at her.

She couldn't hear for the howling of the wind, and the rain beating on the car. Seeing their mouths moving, she got the message. Flinging the door open, they piled in on top of her.

"You're wet!" she objected. "And cold!"

"Move over, Annie. Let them sit down and shut the door before we all drown or get struck by lightning!" Daisy implored.

Legs, arms, jeaned bottoms were topsy-turvy in the back seat.

"Oooooh, Sammy! Your tennis shoes stink!" Annie disgustedly wailed.

"You don't smell so good yourself!" Sammy laughed with gusto as he rubbed a turkey smelling hand over her nose.

"Mama! Make Sammy quit it!" Annie demanded.

"Prissy, Prissy is a little sissy!" taunted Sammy, laughing with true delight at his cousin.

"Ya! She's a sissy!" joined Reginald. "Didn't even dare go out to help us with the turkeys!"

Annie felt indignant. "I'm NOT a sissy. You're just stinky, dumb boys! You don't know anything!" She pushed the offending feet and hands away from her scrunched up nose.

"Okay boys. That's enough," Daisy said. "Here comes Daddy. Open the door for him. Hurry!"

A door was flung open by a wet child hanging over the back seat. Malvern jumped in just as a huge crack of thunder simultaneously crashed with a flash of lightning which lit up the entire area.

"Let's get out of here," Malvern said.

The family breathed a sigh of relief. Anxious for Malvern as he had battled the elements to save his flocks, they had all found a moment in between the teasing to pray for him. None of them would have willingly let him go there alone for anything in the world. They never told him that. He was a quietly proud man. No one needed to baby-sit him, in his estimation.

Finally a clap of ear-splitting thunder heralded the end of the deluge. The sun timidly peeked from behind a sloppy black cloud, and bathed the wet man, car and all within, in feeble sunshine. Rivulets of rain water dripped off the roosts, looking like silver threads in the evening glow. Seated on towels which were draped over a plastic drop cloth, he started the car, turned it around, and onto the field road down which he would check the corn, oats, wheat, red clover, buckwheat and rye.

"Well, praise the Lord," Malvern softly said, "it doesn't look too bad. There are a few downed patches here and there." A broad grin graced his face, and he started to sing, "How Great Thou Art."

Annie thrilled to her father's golden voice. It was as smooth as honey - a deep, rich bass. Daisy started to harmonize with the tune Malvern was singing, then Annie joined in, singing second alto. Jan and Reginald added their equally mellow voices to the mix. "How Great Thou Art," had never had it so good, except when they heard a certain famous singer lovingly sing it at crusades, George Beverly Shea.

Driving back to the house, Malvern, on a whim asked, "Would you all like an ice cream cone?"

"Yes," everyone chorused, including Daisy, who was 'in the way,' (pregnant.)

"Well, then let's go to New York Mills creamery. They have cones with three huge scoops for a nickel apiece!" Malvern exclaimed.

"Hooray!" the kids chorused. At times like this, Russians, bears and stalkers were nonexistent to Annie.

Malvern headed the car down the driveway. As they rounded the woods onto vast fields, a thick, tremendous bolt of lightning blazed from heaven and bored itself miles away into the earth below the deep blue of the western sky.

It bored and bored, seemingly never letting up.

Daisy gasped. "Malvern! That looks like lightning is striking Foerster's farm!"

Malvern said, "Yes, it does. It has hit something." He fell deathly silent, bringing the car to the end of the driveway.

Quietly he pulled to a stop. "Children," he said. "I feel we should pray for Ronald and his parents, right now. Will you join me?"

"Yes, Dad," the children softly chorused, fear in their voices.

"Dear Lord. Please be with that dear family. I don't know how to pray, nor what to ask, but I do thank you that even though adversity be great, You are even greater. You are our strength, and our help in the time of trouble. Please lend them your mighty and powerful strength, and love. Amen."

Annie felt a twinge of dread touch her heart.

"Children, instead of going to our neighboring town, do you mind if we just go one mile into our own little village? We can get ice cream cones there, and I'll throw in a candy bar for each of you, too."

Everyone was thinking the same thing.

"I would like to drive over to the Foerster's right now, once we get your treats. Would that be alright with all of you?"

"Yes, dear," Daisy reached over and took Mal's hand.

"Yes, Dad," Jan said.

"It's fine, Dad. You don't even have to take me to get a treat tonight if you'd like to wait," Reginald offered.

"Daddy, I'm not hungry," Annie said.

Sammy and Cherry agreed.

"Well, then, why don't I take you to Grandma and Grandpa's as planned, where you can get bathed and ready to jump into those famous featherbeds of theirs?" Malvern asked.

"That'd be great!" Annie suddenly wanted the retired easy comfort of her elderly grandparents, and the silliness of Sammy, with Cherry's infectious cheer. She felt that her mother needed to ride together with their father wherever his intuition was taking them.

"Where's Marla?" Jan asked.

"She's spending the night at a friend's" Daisy replied.

"Was it near the lightning bolt - her friend's house?" Annie timidly asked.

"No, darling it's in quite the opposite direction."

*

After tea and cookies at Grandma's, Grandpa Illy put Annie on his knee.

"Grandpa, I'm too big!" Annie laughed.

"No you're not," he said. "You're still quite small for your age. Here. You used to like playing 'to gallop, to gallop.' Let's go!" And, up and down she jogged on his knee, until midst squeals of laughter, he'd almost let her fall to the ground in a grand finale.

"Off to bed you all go," Grandma Illy told her assorted grandchildren. "Go brush your teeth again, and remember, I've put the porcelain potties out for you. There's one in each room." She started to laugh pleasantly, "Just don't try to move them once they've been used," she said. "And, put the lid back on afterward."

Hugging Grandpa around the neck, Annie kissed his white hair. Then she turned to Grandma and looked deep and long into her 'twin's' eyes of green.

"Do you think...?" A pained look came into her face thinking of where her mom and dad had gone.

"Annie. I know. No matter what happens, we know that it will be God's will."

"But Grandma, I don't understand sometimes."

"We don't always know why things

happen, dear. But we do know that the difficult things in life make us strong. If there was always sunshine and no rain, the sweet peas in the flower garden by the shed would never mature to give their beautiful scent, nor to show their lovely garments of delicate hues. <u>We live to become like Jesus</u>. Even He suffered. But, in the end, His suffering stopped, and His Father in heaven gathered Him back where He belonged to make a place for <u>us</u>. It's just as beautiful there as it is here. Isn't it nice to know that when we go from this home to that one, we will be happy?"

"Just like when I come here from Mama and Daddy's?"

"Yes, my little Annie."

"I'm always happy in both places," Annie smiled and hugged her grandmother's neck.

*

The next morning, the telephone rang. Annie lay in Grandma's feather bed beside her sleeping cousin, Cherry, wondering if it was Daisy or Daddy. She softly stole out of bed, and padded down the steps to the fragrant dining room. Her grandmother was sitting at a black oak secretary, looking out the ornate window toward the park where the 'holy ghost' and his family lived (the doves.)

Annie stood quietly in her nightie at her grandmother's side. Grandmother lifted her eye-glasses and wiped the corners of her lovely eyes. Then her right arm reached out for Annie. She drew the child close to herself.

"Annie, darling," she softly began. "I have something to tell you which will bring you great pain. But, you must be a big girl, and remember that sometimes God gives us a person who is <u>so</u> good and beautiful in every way, that God Himself wants the pleasure of that one's company." She turned to look Annie full in the face. Putting her other arm around the girl also, she lifted her upon the welcoming knees Annie had grown to love through the years.

"Darling, last evening God walked through His garden and picked the most beautiful flower He could find for His own, heavenly bouquet." She gathered Annie's blond head to her shoulder, holding her tight...so tightly that Annie felt the sensation that nothing could ever rip her from the safety of her grandmother's arms, her voice, her wisdom, her knowing of all things.

Annie felt something wet soak through her hair on the top of her little head. It was her grandmother's silent tears.

"My precious namesake. That beautiful flower whom God chose to honor with His heaven was our dear friend, Ronald Foerster. On the way to safety from the storm last evening, he was struck by lightning. He was on a tractor, coming in from the fields."

Annie never could remember what

happened immediately after she heard that. All she could remember was that days later, Grandma invited her to come in for a special low tea. Annie was given her favorite nosegay of pink, white and lavender sweet peas from the garden. It graced the snowy linen tablecloth in Grandma's cool dining room. Annie was served from her favorite Havilland China teapot, teacup and saucer. She remembered Ronald while sadly watching the goldfish swim in their sparkling bowl 'neath the fern by the window. For some reason, the cookies didn't taste good that day, nor the finger sandwiches Grandma had made her. She didn't care if there was sugar in her cup of tea or not. When Grandma asked, "What may I do for you, dear?" Annie asked, "Would you walk with me to the church? Please, may I see Ronald again?"

"Yes, I will walk through the park to the church with you, sweetheart." She pulled Annie into her arms. "But, we can't see Ronald, for he is already in heaven with our heavenly Father."

"Isn't there anything left? Not even his guitar?"

"Yes, his guitar is here, at his mom and dad's. And, when we stand outside the church, we will see a beautiful pink velvet bed in which his sleeping body will wait for the coming of the Lord."

"What will happen then, Grandma?" Annie asked.

"Well, the Bible says that the dead in Christ shall rise and be joined to their spirits once more. Ronald, as we've known him, will ascend into heaven wherever that may be."

"Daddy said that being with God <u>is</u> heaven. Is it Grandma?"

"Yes, child. Yes, it is."

"And Ronald is with God now?" Annie got off the dining room chair. "Then he is happy, I think." Annie put her hand in Grandma Anne's and they left to walk through the park toward the church.

"Grandma."

"Yes, Annie?"

"After the stalker chased me, Ronald

came to sing. He stayed at our house for supper. A few nights later, I dreamed that he was an angel. He had a white robe and soft, white wings. Jesus was there, and they were friends. Ronald played his guitar for Jesus and sang, too."

"Then it must bring a good feeling to know that that is exactly where he is and what he's doing now. Does it, dear?" Grandma squeezed Annie's hand lovingly.

"Yes, but it still aches in here," Annie pressed her right hand against her chest. "It hurts and feels full. I want to just lie down and cry, Grandma." Tears poured down her plump cheeks. "When will I feel better? I don't even like cherry dropths anymore." Her lisp had returned.

"It will be painful for some time to come whenever you think of him. We like to be with the ones we love, you see." The older woman put her arm across the little shoulders of her granddaughter.

They walked in silence and then stood to watch the mourners file from the church behind a pink velvet, elongated box. Annie struggled to keep from running to her weeping Sunday School teacher who was right behind the casket of her only son. Wanting to throw her arms around Mrs. Foerster, the child yearned to tell her that she loved her; and that right now Ronald was in heaven's Angels and Guitars band, playing for Jesus!

"Goodbye, angel," Annie whispered as a long, low gray car carrying the strange bed inside, pulled away from the village church.

For the first time, a lasting hush fell on the girl's spirit which made her feel compassion for the anguish of others. Losing Ronald made her appreciate the physicality of those around her. She now treasured most things about others which made them different from herself, for she knew that their differences were God's gift to all.

Holding hands, Grandma and Annie passed flower beds of white and red bleeding hearts in the park, as the woman quietly spoke of someone she had loved in the long ago.

"Darling. The parting of friends, whether by this kind of death or the kind brought on by suddenly disappearing into thin air once you say goodbye, hurts just the same. I had a friend named Little Fawn when I was your age. Our two nations were enemies, but her dad and mine liked each other. Instead of separating us by hateful stories, they helped us meet because all we saw, was another little girl. She taught me to speak Ogalala Sioux. I taught her English. Our dads knew we all had to learn to get along in order to form a secure, strong country when people my age became adults." Grandma cleared her throat and continued.

"Little Fawn and I loved each other so much, we became blood sisters." Anne's eyes searched the sky.

"One day her papa and uncles met my pa and me. The rules from Washington said that their entire band, plus all the others across the United States had to go live on government-given property called Reservations. So, we were brought to one another to say goodbye. I wept. She wept. I never saw, nor heard of her again until after you were born. I thought she had died during the harsh Dakotah Plains winters." Grandmother Anne's steps slowed.

"Oddly, my last child, your mother Daisy, looked exactly like Little Fawn as she grew to nine years old. I found great comfort in that."

Annie looked up at Granny. The lady peered down at her and said, "Anyway, she didn't perish. I saw her seven years ago in Sioux City. She lives on the Winnebago Reservation. She has a granddaughter your age who goes to the Indian school nearby in St. Francis, South Dakota, where your Aunt Abbey teaches."

Mrs. Illy fell silent. Then in a soft voice she said, "Time heals hurts, sweetheart. Remember that."

Annie had never heard such a long spiel out of her grandma before. But, she was fascinated by it especially when the former 'Little Nettie' took her upstairs, opened the huge steamer trunk and pulled out a beautiful, soft doeskin dress embroidered with colorful porcupine quills with a bag to match. The fringe on the garment tickled Annie's swollen-from-crying nose when Grandmother helped her put it on; and the fur in the matching winter moccasins felt soft as a bunny, for that is what lined them on the inside – white rabbit fur.

"You sure know how to make a kid feel better, Grandma!" Annie said as she preened before the mirror. "Do you think Ronald can see me now?"

Chapter 7

Everlasting Tea

The next morning broke upon a dark and gloomy sky full of clouds as thick as a soldier's battle helmet. Annie sat on the floor in the east bedroom looking forlornly through the sheers at the promise of a rainy day. Suddenly, to cheer her, the dew drops on the grass started to sparkle when clouds, parted by a flashing sword of sunshine, lost their bullet aspect.

A winsome smile pulled at the corners of her mouth as she wondered if the sun shone all the time in heaven where Ronald was. She said aloud, "I wonder what you are having for breakfast today, angel." Supposing that people in heaven ate off tables of golden linen instead of white damask like the setting in her own dining room, she thought, 'I like the white better,' got up, and went downstairs to find the table already set with fork to the left of the plate on which was a smaller plate holding a cereal bowl, knife and spoons to the right (and in that order), glass at the exact tip of the knife, tea cup and saucer to the right of the spoons where one could easily take hold of the handle. The sun was spilling its joy over the sparkling place settings for eight people.

"Are Cherry and Sammy coming for breakfast, Mama?" She spoke softly at her parents closed bedroom door which was ten extra steps from the table as one passed from it, to and through the corner of the living room.

Her mother, hearing an unmistakably sad note in the daughter's voice, said, "Yes, dear. Then we're all going to take Sammy to the bus station in Wahpeton. He's going back to Nebraska today."

"Oh, Mama!" Annie turned round, ran

upstairs, threw herself onto the bed, and cried into her pillow.

"Dear Jesus, why is everyone I love leaving all at once?" she asked of her Best Friend. "First you decided to invite Ronald to everlasting tea; and now you're letting Sammy go home already. Don't you care about me at all? For someone being in charge of my happiness, it seems to me that you don't know me very well!" She cried more. "What if someone had jerked your cousin away from you just when your friend died?" She wiped the tears from her lips. They tasted too salty. "Once I heard Daddy say that a friend of his had rotten timing. Well, I think you do too!"

Suddenly fear struck her heart because she realized she was talking naughtily to gentle Jesus. 'After all,' she thought, 'I shouldn't talk to you like this after what you've done for me - dying on the cross and being wrapped in a pile of clean rags before they stuck you in a tomb. Gosh! That must have been scary! I'm sure glad you got out of there in a hurry!'

"Well, at least Sammy isn't dead. He will be back next summer, I know. He always comes. Cherry, too," she said and got onto her knees beside the bed asking the Lord to forgive her outburst. Annie prayed, "I'm saclamidjous (sacrilegious). Mama said so! She says that I am irreversed (irreverent) sometimes, Jesus. I'm sorry. I'll try harder next time. It isn't easy being a kid. You know that. Daddy said you were one once and even ran away from your mom and dad. I've never been that bad! So, I guess we're even. Right ?"

The girl felt peace steal over her heart after reconciling herself to God's obvious will via her aunt and uncle's choice for their boy. Sammy must go home.

Annie went downstairs again for breakfast where she found the rest of the family waiting for her.

"Here comes Grandpa's car," she sounded the death knell of her summertime fun. Mama and Daddy looked at each other across the table as he rose to greet the cousins and his in-laws.

*

After seeing Sammy off on the bus, which had a white rabbit painted on its blue side, Mama, Cherry and Annie rode back across the flat Red River Valley of the North to the rolling hills which seemed to converge at the county seat of Fergus Falls, "Glaciers carved these hills and flatlands as they slid through, millions of years ago," Malvern had informed the kids.

Pulling alongside the curb in front of the optician's store, Grandma got out of the car and went in to pick up her glasses. After coming back to the gang, she asked, "How would everyone like a little lunch?"

"Hooray!" Annie piped.

Cherry laughed and started climbing out of the DeSoto saying, "And we're off! Like a herd of turtles!"

She and Annie walked down the street as fast as they could without running. (They were required to act ladylike.)

"Girls, wait!" Daisy called softly; for ladies refrained from raising their voices at all times whether in or out of one's home. Children's ears were tuned to softness, even exuberantly so.

The girls stopped, and started looking at hats in the milliner's shop window.

"Let's go in here, first, Ma," Daisy said as the women came abreast of the eight and eleven year old cousins. "I need a new hat for church. Look at that sharp little number...the black straw with white piping and three blanc ostrich plumes. Isn't that adorable?"

"Yes, it is. Why, I think you'd look pretty in it, Daisy," Grandmother Anne agreed. "You'll look as if you're wearing the Prince of Wales feathers!" She smiled and opened the door for her obviously 'with child' daughter as Daisy laughed joyously. Her black hair shone blue in the sun, along with that of her mother's. Their earrings and hats fit them well, and Grandmother's diamond ring caught the sun in its prisms, sending a flash of light into Annie's green eyes. Forever after, Annie would love diamonds and white ostrich plumes.

Soon Daisy and Grandmother were being waited upon by two milliners, who left Cherry and Annie to examine the merchandise.

"This is a hat heaven!" Annie whispered in Cherry's ear.

"It sure is," Cherry whispered enthusiastically.

Picking a black bowler off a hat stand, she looked furtively toward Daisy and her grandmother. Annie and Cherry ducked down to be less obvious while Cherry put the nearly rimless felt bucket, sprouting five long, brown feathers, on her head.

Annie almost shouted with laughter when, instead of sitting prettily on Cherry's head, it fell clear to her nose. The pheasant feathers caused it to tilt forward, striking the eight year old in the face.

"What the...?" Cherry tried to pull it off, but it got stuck on her pony tail. Cherry started to laugh while Annie clapped her hand over her own mouth to stifle uncontrollable giggles. Cherry had always seemed so cosmopolitan, and here was Annie's idol harpooned by a hat!

"Annie! Do something!" Cherry whispered. "HELP me before Grandma finds us!" Her infectious laughter couldn't be stopped.

Suddenly a movement caught Annie's eye. The clerk was walking down the aisle toward them.

"Get down!" Annie grabbed Cherry's shoulders and pulled her off the vanity stool. Quickly shoving her cousin head first into a space reserved for ladies knees, Cherry's head collided with the backboard crumpling the feathers and all, molding the hat to her face. The new hapless knight couldn't see without a movable visor.

"Annie, what are you doing? Where am I?" she kept laughing.

"Be quiet!" Annie hissed, poking her

knees into Cherry's body as she hurriedly sat on the bench facing the mirror to hide her cohort and the crumpled chapeau.

Trying on an innocent looking yellow straw she whispered, "Shhh! Here comes the hat lady."

"Hello dear," the storekeeper smiled. "Have you found something you'd like your mother to see? I'll call her over here for you, if you wish."

"Oh, thank you, but," Annie stuttered, turning pink as a 'sailors take warning' sunrise. "I don't like this one." She took it off her head, hoping that the lady would go away so Cherry could get out from under the vanity. The looking glass was quivering from Cherry's efforts to stifle.

"That's no problem, dear," the lady answered. "We have a cute little felt over in aisle four. I'll be right back with it. Then you can try it on." The woman walked away.

"Cherry! Cherry! Get out of there!" Annie started pulling her cousin's skirt. "You've got to hurry! She's coming back!"

Cherry backed out on all fours. Annie took hold of Cherry's head, stuck her pudgy fingers under the rim of the squashed bowler and mortified feathers. Putting her foot against Cherry's shoulder, she pulled with all her might.

"Here, dear," the attendant called. "I found it," and high heels started clack, clack, clacking toward Annie and her erstwhile cousin.

"Hurry, Annie!" Cherry giggled.

"I'm TRYING!" Annie tugged and tugged.

"Oh, Ma'am, could you come and help me for a moment?" they heard Daisy inquire of the owner of the clackety shoes.

"Yes, of course," a mild voice responded as the click-clack started receding toward a different area of the store.

Wide-eyed, the girls breathed a sigh of relief.

"Can't you get this off?" Cherry was on her knees as if in supplication to the Almighty, hands to her head, trying to help Annie. "What's stuck in the back? It'll pull my pony tail off, not to mention my whole head!" Her voice rolled with laughter.

"Quit making me laugh," Annie giggled. "When I count to three, you push up on the sides of your head, and I'll pull toward me from the back by your pony tail."

"Okay," Cherry counted "one, two, thuuureeee!"

The hat came off with a vengeance, sending Annie sprawling backwards into a high stand, its shelves full of millinery delights which came showering upon her, one finally landing smack on her braids.

"Oh," Cherry laughed. "Land-o-Goshen! Are we in for it now!" She threw the smashed helmet with its broken, rag-tag feathers into the corner behind a dust bin, straightened her hair, smoothed her skirt and turned to face whatever it was that was sounding like an army marching on the double toward them.

"What is happening?" Grandmother quietly asked, suddenly materializing before them. Surrounded by three Amazon ladies, she looked corsetedly maternal.

The two owners opened their mouths to scold, but Grandma's soothing voice continued, "Why, Annie, that selection you've made looks wonderful on you!" She laughed good-naturedly. "In your enthusiasm, did you back into the hats?"

The matriarch of the family set to work picking toppers off the floor, blowing each one and delicately brushing it with her capable, square little hands. Deftly arranging them on the shelves, the store was in order in no time, as were the jangled nerves of the storekeepers and Daisy.

Two hats were purchased at the register; and an invitation to peruse for selections of the next season's delights was accepted by the satisfied customers.

"Grandma and Auntie will never know about the black bowler, will they?" Cherry whispered to Annie as they walked down Main Street, swinging a yellow hat between them.

Hot roast beef sandwiches and mashed potatoes with gravy had no trouble going down minutes later. The piece de resistance, apple pie ala mode which followed, rounded out the lunch Grandmother Anne bought everyone.

"You make good memories, Grandma," Annie smiled. "Thank you, and thanks for rescuing us from the crabby clerks."

Her comfort zone laughed quietly. "You are welcome, young lady. I bet you'll be a little more careful next time, won't you?" She jiggled from chuckles. "My! But you looked comical sitting on the floor in your new cowgirl hat!" She stirred cream into her coffee, and set the teaspoon carefully onto the saucer which held the cup. "When you want something, you really go after it, don't you!"

Daisy started to laugh. "Actually, we paid for three hats, Ma."

"Yes, Annie's, mine and," she pulled something out of a flowered paper bag — "Cherry's!"

Annie burst into laughter at the sight of the squashed felt helmet replete with broken pheasant feathers sticking out in all directions.

"Where'd you get that?" Cherry gasped.

"Oh, Cherry?" Grandmother chortled, looking over her bifocals at a very red granddaughter as she plopped it on her own head.

"Oh, lordy, Grandma," Cherry was giggling so hard she couldn't continue. Annie had slumped down in the booth holding her sides.

"Sit up, Annie. Don't be so loud!" Daisy implored.

Annie sat up, put her hand over her mouth and subdued her laughter, eyes merry and bright.

"Well," Cherry tried again, "it was like this..."

A few minutes later a happy foursome returned over hills and streams, motoring in a green car on a black highway to their own village and farm.

For one whole afternoon, Annie had forgotten the summer's baptism into another reality. During the summer she had experienced forgiveness without lasting bitterness; awareness without fear, and death of a friend with the hope of eternal, happy life with God. The sweet Christ who had come into her heart when she accepted Him, made that possible. For, in so doing, Annie released the greatest magic in the world - Christ's love and the power of His name, Jesus. When she called on Him, He saved her from harm and lasting trauma. The young girl discovered it true what her dad said: "Greater is He (Jesus) that is within you, than he (Satan) that is in the world." (I John 4:4.)

As the car turned into the Cumming's driveway Annie asked Daisy, "Remember when Ronald came to play the guitar and sing about the Lord after Jesus sent Daddy to catch the bad man?"

"Yes," her mom replied.

"Well, how is it that when I prayed to Jesus, God's only forgotten Son..."

"Not forgotten, dear. Begotten," Mother interjected.

"Whatever," Annie dismissed the correction. "The prayer was answered as if I had prayed to His Dad. His Dad is God of everything! Isn't His name, Jehovah?"

"Whoa! Slow down! One question at a time," her mom laughed. "Yes, His Dad's name is Jehovah, amongst other names. Most languages have their own name for Father God." She cast a bemused look at her youngest child.

"Secondly," Daisy continued, "Jesus is everything His Dad is. He said, 'I and my Father are One. He who has seen me has seen the Father.'"

"Is that why Jesus can answer prayer?" the little blond wanted to know.

"Precisely," Daisy answered

"I know He said that because it's in red ink in my Bible," Annie offered. "I read all the red words and skip the rest because the black are boring."

"My goodness, child." Daisy pulled the car up to the garage and turned off the engine. "Come on," she invited, "let's carry our new hats into the house; and make supper."

As they walked toward the door, Annie said, "Just think, Mama. Someday I will tell other boys and girls in Africa about Jesus and His Father!"

Daisy said, "You really want to become a missionary, don't you!"

"I love Jesus a lot, Mama," the girl soberly looked up at her mom. "He's always with me."

"'Yes,' He said, 'I am with you even unto the end of the world.'"

Daisy patted her daughter's upturned collar back into place.

The End